Caroline Pitcher

Caroline Pitcher lives in Derbyshire with her husband, daughter, son and lots of animals and birds. She taught in London for thirteen years and now writes down most things that come into her head. Her first novel, *Diamond*, won the Kathleen Fidler Award and *Kevin the Blue* was the 1993 Independent Story of the Year. Caroline's picture book, *The Snow Whale*, has been shortlisted for the Children's Book Award.

Also in the Contents series

Mine

Caroline Pitcher

Caroline Pitcher

To les and Jean with love
from Caroline, October 1997

mammoth

First published in Great Britain in 1997 by Mammoth
an imprint of Reed International Books Ltd
Michelin House, 81 Fulham Road, London SW3 6RB
and Auckland and Melbourne

Copyright © 1997 Caroline Pitcher

The moral rights of the author and cover illustrator
have been asserted

ISBN 0 7497 2875 2

10 9 8 7 6 5 4 3 2 1

A CIP catalogue record for this title
is available from the British Library

Typeset by Avon Dataset Ltd, Bidford on Avon, B50 4JH
Printed in Great Britain by Cox & Wyman Ltd, Reading, Berkshire

for my dear friend
Maggie MacKechnie

One

When Shelley Taylor was a little girl she sometimes heard voices. The voices had no faces or mouths that she could see.

'I can't hear all the words they say,' she told her father. 'The voices have no middles. But I know they want me to listen to them. They go on at me, and they won't stop.'

'Don't listen,' said her father. 'And don't tell anyone what you hear. They'll think you're mad.'

So, after that, if Shelley thought a voice was hovering near her, waiting for a listener, she covered up her ears and walked away. This didn't always work.

Now, all this time later, Shelley became aware of a soft clamouring in her head. It was late December. Shelley was seventeen, and living without her father now, in a muddle of a village clinging to the side of a narrow dale in Derbyshire. The dale was dim and secret as the fold in an elbow. A whisper here would be too loud.

The voice that was waiting for Shelley didn't know how to whisper.

She knew it was hiding somewhere, waiting for her. That's why she hadn't stayed in the cottage alone. She had gone out to walk the steep lanes and yards and jitties, around the houses and barns crouched round the squat church. Now she was outside the cottage again, searching for her keys.

The mist drew back.

She let herself in to the cottage, closed the storm door and then the inner door firmly after her, turned to cross to the stairs, and it got her.

'Ere! Listen, will yer? Will yer? If yer'll only listen . . .'

'No!' cried Shelley and turned back across the room. Immediately there was a knock on the front door.

Shelley held her breath. The knock came again. She waited for that nagging voice. Nothing. She went to lift the inner door latch and saw that the storm door now stood ajar. She knew she had closed it.

'Hello?' she whispered. She stepped into the porch and peered around the doorframe, right into a man's face. He was young, perhaps a few years older than Shelley, and just a little taller. His eyes shone like jet. A sheepdog stood motionless by his heel.

'Er – Mrs Taylor?' he said.

'No. That's my mother,' said Shelley. 'Clare Taylor. Though she may not be Taylor much longer.'

'Oh.' The young man's face puckered in confusion. He glanced

2

down. Over his arm, like a waiter, he was carrying linen. 'They're for the bathroom,' he said. 'And there's a clean tablecloth for the house. It's Mrs Harvey has sent them round.' His voice was low and Shelley had to listen hard to make out what he said. 'I thought I'd catch you in the street, but you were too fast for me.'

'Thank you,' said Shelley, holding out both arms. He placed the towels and tablecloth awkwardly over them, as if Shelley were a clothes dryer.

'Mrs Harvey's my mother,' he said. 'It's her cottage.'

'Oh.'

'I'm Matthew Harvey,' he said, as if she would want to know. 'You're here for a while?'

Go away, she wanted to say, but she stayed silent.

'You've picked a raw time of year to come. We get every bit of weather in this village. We're so high up here, see, no shelter from the north. It's not much of a holiday up here just now.'

'We're not on holiday.' Shelley was getting more irritated.

'Oh?' he said, waiting, insistent.

Shelley wasn't going to look at him. He had never heard of cool. He was nosey and intrusive, nothing guarded, no dissembling.

'Well then. We live there, Linnet Farm. Up there.' He pointed up the hill. Shelley saw a tall farmhouse, built in the local grey-brown limestone, leaning over the street. Its narrow windows stared blankly down at the cottage.

'If you want anything, just come up,' he said. She felt him watching her until she had to look at him, into his eyes as dark as the treacle her mother had poured into the cake at Christmas. 'You a student?' he asked.

'No, but I will be soon,' she said. Three Ds, that's all she needed to get, they'd told her, then away to university at last, right away to a new start. To Oxford, away from her family, away from here and away from these voices that worried round her head like bees. Especially that one waiting for her in the cottage . . . So there, Derbyshire farm lad in your overalls and wellingtons!

'Great,' he said. 'See you, then.' And he strode away from her up the hill, heavy-footed in his big boots, thick dark hair frizzled in the damp air. 'Like a scouring pad,' she said to herself. She watched him all the way up the hill. He didn't look back.

She was just about to go back inside when she heard someone shuffling up the street towards her. It was an old man in a tartan dressing-gown. He was bent as a croquet hoop and he had trodden down the backs of his slippers so that they flopped between his feet and the cobblestones. A cat crouched in the gutter, fixated by the flopping sound. The old man's head twisted round out of his shoulders. His soft mouth gaped. He stopped to stare at Shelley.

Her cheeks burned as she stumbled back inside, closing the storm door and then the inner door firmly after her. She stooped to peep through the window. The old man was waiting, head cocked, listening. Then he set off again, flip-flapping on his way.

Shelley put the neatly-ironed tablecloth and the little stack of tea towels on the sideboard, and turned round slowly, ready to jump at that voice, but this time the voice was silent.

The cottage was so prettified, so self-consciously softened with chintzy fabrics and dried flowers and glass dishes of potpourri, as if the decor could compensate for the bleakness of the land all around. There was a fire laid in the neat little grate. By it stood a basket filled with designer logs, silver-skinned wrapping wood, pale as honey, regularly dusted. The fire in the grate was laid with real logs, dark, powdery and worm-eaten.

Each of the three low bedrooms had an electric storage heater and there was another in the kitchen, yet the cottage felt damp. Ever since they had arrived, Shelley's brother, Adam, had been burning his birth sign incense sticks to cover up the damp smell. 'Aries, the very first sign of the zodiac!' he'd shouted. 'Bold, courageous and powerful! Adventurous yet playful, that's me, Aries Man! The Derby Ram in Reeboks!' And then he had posed, incense stick outstretched, as if it were the torch borne by the Olympic messenger.

He made her sick.

Like Adam, the incense was overpowering.

Shelley went through in to the bathroom. The bath suite was sugared-almond pink, the thick towels Matthew had given her white with a pink trim and appliquéd roses. 'This bathroom has been added on,' said her mother scornfully. 'I bet they never got planning permission.'

The cottage was built of stone. One part of the little window at the north end had been filled in. 'That's someone trying not to pay window tax,' her mother had said, in a voice smug with knowledge. 'Eighteenth century, I should think. And there may have been stone stairs before the wooden ones. The limestone would wear away and dip and crumble, I suppose. Mmm. There's what looks like a false wall round the other side. I wonder if they blocked the old stairs off . . .'

Now her mother was out with Adam and Dave.

Shelley wanted to be safely alone in her bedroom before they came back. To get there, she had to brave the stairs. She took a deep breath and opened the door. The stairwell was narrow as a chimney and here was another smell, a sour-sweet cloud of something dank, decaying, like a marsh. No one else had remarked on it yet, not Adam or Dave, not even Shelley's fussy mother.

Perhaps it's just for me, thought Shelley gloomily. It was so strong, like liquid cheese. Adam's incense could never take on this one.

The polished wooden steps were shiny and treacherous and Shelley put the palm of her hand against the wall which ran by the side. She felt the damp seeping back towards her. The stone took the water inside itself and hid it.

'Here goes,' Shelley whispered, ready to dash, but it was too late. The voice had found her again.

'Ere! Will yer listen? Will yer?

Nowt to do but sit 'ere, crammed agin this stair.
Nowt to do but hide . . . Will yer listen? Will yer?'

'I won't listen to you!' cried Shelley and she tore up the stairs, ducking the beam at the top. She threw herself into the little bedroom and scrabbled for cotton wool in her drawer and stuffed a wodge into each ear. She was free again, for a while at least, from that shrill nagging voice!

She scowled round the room, at the frilly pillowcases and flowery valance, at the white embroidered cotton on the dressing-table. She hated all this nostalgic decor, Laura Ashley on the cheap. When they moved to the new house she would have black and gold in her room, plain and dramatic, style not fuss.

Shelley knelt before the small window. It was mullioned in gritstone and set in a wall thick as a fortress to beat back the winter winds. She touched the festoon of curtains, rosebuds dancing on a buttermilk background. Between their frills hung a further curtain of snow-white lace.

'What are you *for*, curtain?' she asked it. 'There's no one out there on the hill. Any dirty voyeur would freeze to death. There's only sheep to watch me undress and I don't suppose they've got binoculars.' She lifted the curtain wire off the hook at each end and placed it on the thick sill. The lace curtain spilled over the edge like whipped milk.

Now the little world outside the window sat in a frame for her to see. There was a field of brownish-yellow grass edged by a dry-stone wall. Where the wall had collapsed, there stood an iron bedstead to block the gap. Beyond the wall a hill rose steeply, littered with stones and scrub. 'It's a lead-miners' hill,' her mother had said. 'Not exactly picturesque, is it?'

Along the top of the hill ran a crest of trees, sticking out as thick and black as chimney-sweeps' brushes. Those trees look like a Mohican haircut, she thought.

It was the day after Boxing Day, one of those days lost between Christmas and New Year, days without names. There were no leaves, no flowers, no woods that Shelley could see, no glossy evergreens, and no hedgerows to promise white blossom frothing on black twigs in spring. Little earth here, only stone. The turf barely covered the rock, which was pale as bone, round as a skull.

As Shelley knelt before the window that December afternoon she thought she could hear water. It ran under the earth, flowing through underground springs as if they were capillaries, hair-thin. It soaked and clotted and lay cradled in stone. The water was so strong. In the distance, Shelley heard deep water swell and settle, stirring over the rock and under the wind's breath. It never soaked quite away, like the voices. And she heard them again, one distant, like a bird twittering high out of sight, but one much nearer, harsh as a crow. It had followed her.

'Ere, I'm Joan. Joanie, me Fayther an me three brothers call me. They call me Fat Joanie. An I'll tell yer why I'm stook down 'ere, if yer'll only listen to me . . .'

Two

Shelley slammed the door shut. She secured the latch and sank on to the bed.

The other voices were so faint. They called and waited. Perhaps they drifted from the water, the huge reservoir which had been built beyond the hills to catch water for the cities. It must be the people sailing and windsurfing, the instructors calling, the children scrambling up rigging and whizzing down slides in the adventure playground, or dashing over to grab for themselves a swing suddenly empty.

Strange how sound travels, thought Shelley, the landscape throws the sounds out of sequence and disembodies them, so that they're distorted on the journey through the hills and dales towards me.

The voices came nearer.

'Leave me alone!' she cried. But here they were.

'Cooo-ooo! Shell-eee!'

A hoot of her mother's laughter, Dave's low murmur. Then a blast from the television, her brother, Adam, flicking from channel to channel at full volume; football, the gloomy music from *EastEnders*, police sirens and American shouting. Television off, a brief respite before the manic merry tunes of his Gameboy.

Adam the Annoyer. Adam the Appendage. Adam the Irritant.

Shelley watched the latch twitching as her mother struggled at the top of the stairs. The door opened, her mother almost swinging into her room on it, pink-faced, wanting to talk.

With a long-suffering sigh, Shelley took the cotton wool from her ears. It hadn't kept out the voice in the cottage or the voices from beyond the hill, and it certainly wouldn't muffle her mother.

'There you are, Shelley, love!' As if it was a surprise to find her. 'You should have come with us, Shelley. It's quite pleasant, the pub, it's not just olde-worlde rubbish and dusty corn-dollies. There's a good fire, and food, and a nice children's room.'

'I'm seventeen.'

'Shelley, I didn't mean – of course you're too old. I forget.' Her mother glanced round the tiny room. 'I thought I heard you talking to someone,' she said suspiciously. Her eyes met Shelley's briefly, then she looked away. Her nose made that little sideways twitch Shelley saw too often, like a rabbit trying to make sense of its surroundings.

'No, I'm not talking to anyone,' said Shelley. 'I don't see how you could have heard anyway, you all made so much noise when you came in. Good job I wasn't trying to sleep.'

'Why, aren't you feeling well, are you starting your period?'

'No-o! Why do you always say that? Eugh, Mother dear, I can smell the gin on you!'

'No, you can't because I had vodka,' said her mother with satisfaction. 'Shelley...'

'What?'

'Please try to enjoy yourself, love. You're still angry, aren't you?'

'About Dad? It's not anger,' said Shelley, staring out at the hillside, willing herself to beam out END OF CONVERSATION, MOTHER.

But her mother took no notice. 'Try not to be too cross,' she said. She spread her hands, palms uppermost and said, 'It's ... it's difficult. His other children are so little. He must have thought you would be bored. Christmases are different when children are only – what are they, seven and four maybe? I tell you, darling, it would have been damn hard work spending Christmas there. Not much sleep for a start.'

'It would have been nice to be asked!' said Shelley.

'He didn't ask Adam either, love. And, in any case, I...'

'Adam was younger when you split up,' cried Shelley. 'It was different for me.'

'You don't have to remind me,' said her mother stiffly. 'I got it all. You were a right little vixen, Shelley.'

'So you keep on telling me. If you'd been an eighteenth century wife you wouldn't have got divorced so easily. You should read the social history I'm doing, see what women had to put up with then. You'd still be with Dad, you'd have had no money.'

'Oh! Oh! Of course, it's *my* fault. I stand rebuked!' cried her mother. 'You don't know the half of it, Shelley. For a while, after Declan left me and cleared off, I thought I might die. I hoped he'd die, too. There! But I learned I could survive anything. And now I have Dave and life is a hundred times happier than it ever was before. I feel I can trust life now.'

'Lucky you.'

'Shelley. Look at you, retreating as far as ever you can. You'll fall through the window in a minute! You're like a crab, creeping away from me, amassing your little stores of stones and shells, sealing yourself in behind them.'

'I like my peace. You know that. You lot, you're so loud! You invade my space. I need to retreat, but you just follow me!'

Her mother plunged her hands into her hair and rolled her eyes. 'For God's sake, Shelley, it's not all doom and gloom. Stop trying to make it so! Stop acting like a lamb to the slaughter!'

Crabs and lambs, Mother. Mixing metaphors this afternoon, aren't you? thought Shelley. She stared pointedly out of the window.

For years after the divorce her mother had dogged Shelley. She picked on her about every dropped sock. She moaned every time Shelley got up too early, whingeing that Shelley had disturbed her own fitful sleep. She moaned every time Shelley slept in late and didn't come down to face the accusing packet of Coco Pops still waiting on the table at twelve. She made sly little insinuations, that Shelley never brought friends home, and wasn't invited to sleep-overs. Shelley didn't *have* proper friends. She felt the other girls watching her, saw their white moons of faces from the corner of her eye. They thought she was weird, she knew, because she passed exams and got good marks, and spent so much time alone. Perhaps in some way they sensed she was different, sensed she heard the voices . . . a loony.

In those long years Shelley read and read, partly because she loved books, but also to avoid having to talk to her mother. And her mother resented Shelley's books. Whenever Shelley just wanted to lie and read, falling thankfully into some fictional world, or history, her mother broke the spell like a petulant child, whining, 'You never stop reading. It would be nice if you looked at me sometimes, Shelley. It'd be nice to be talked to!'

Shelley didn't want to talk to her. It was like walking bare-toed on hot sand. Now Shelley watched her mother fiddling with the lace curtain.

'Look, Shelley,' her mother said, scrunching it in both fists, 'I'm not trying to defend Declan. I know how thoughtless he can be, believe me. But – ' she made her voice softer, 'please put him out of your head. Dave's lighting a fire. I'm going to cook a curry. We're going to have a nice few days here. The builders'll be another few weeks on the new house, but we can get to know the village before you go back to school. You don't need Declan, believe me.'

'Mmmm,' sniffed Shelley, looking away from her mother's expectant face. She knew there would be either hurt, or accusation, probably both, in the green eyes.

Shelley's eyes were green too, but her mother's eyes had crow's feet fanning out from the side, and little hammocks of flesh slung underneath which were much worse if she'd been crying. At one time drink smoothed them out for a while, but they were back again the next day. Yet the green still shone clear as glass, deep in the soft hollows.

Those first years after her father had left, her mother had driven all her anger at Shelley like some terrible medieval weapon, but now there was only an occasional foray, because now there was Dave, even-tempered Dave. It was better now her mother had Dave, better for everyone.

There was still Adam of course . . . Dave and Mum thought he was marvellous! 'I just can't keep a straight face,' was what Shelley had heard all her life whenever Adam did something irritating, something that put him in the limelight. Her mother had never been able to tell him off properly, however hard she sucked in her cheeks to control her giggles.

'Shelley, try to make the best of it. Try to be happy, love . . .' her mother pleaded. She hesitated, then went downstairs.

Shelley sat by the window, listening, until it was dark. She stretched and stood up, wanting the brightness of the fire downstairs. Quick, before Joan senses, but still that smell waited for her, jumped out from somewhere behind the stairs. Parmesan, she thought, cold sick, that's what it is, quick, don't listen, she'll get you! Joan will get you.

But it wasn't Joan, not this time.

'Hey, it's wafer-thin,' said an Al Capone voice. 'Turn sideways,

Shell babe, and you disappear from view! Can't get my sights round you.'

'Shut up, Adam,' she spat.

'Who needs a credit card, babe? I could slip a lock with you any day. The boobless beauty,' he cried. 'Flat as a — '

It was months since Shelley had resorted to physical violence, but halfway up this slippery stair he lost his footing and she had him. She pinched him as viciously as she could, shoved him hard against the stone wall. She put her face right up to his. He wouldn't look frightened, would he? Just laughter in his blue eyes, with their speckles of gold. Like Dad's eyes. His earring glinted below the wild thatch of hair. She wanted to pull it, hard! Rip his ear! Instead she pushed him away again and he clattered up the stairs, shrieking with laughter.

She shouted, 'You're lucky, Dogbreath, I'd really do you over but I can't stand the stink on these stairs. Smells like sick, it's not just damp here. It's not you is it?'

Adam turned to her, his head down to mind the ceiling, and frowned. 'What smell? There's no smell, only potpourri in the sitting room. You're going doolally, Shelley.'

Don't go, please don't go. I don't want to sit by misen, I'm cowd, I want to be in th'ouse with the smoke potherin' and fire burnin'. Is it Childermas agin? Unluckiest day of the year, it is. Unlucky for me, it were . . .

*

No, Joan, thought Shelley, I don't want your story now. I don't like the sound of it. I'm going to sit by the fire without you, and eat curry.

Three

Mrs Harvey hurried in front of Shelley across the yard and in to the barn. Inside it was dim and the smell of hay was clover-sweet. Here and there among the bales Shelley saw brown hens settled like tea cosies. Mrs Harvey reached up into secret nests and brought down eggs to fill the box.

'I'll give these a quick wash before you take them,' she said. 'How are you getting on at the cottage?' She glanced over her shoulder. 'Is it quiet enough for you?'

In the yard beyond them a bull with a back broad as a refectory table bellowed lengthily. His eyes were pink-rimmed as if he'd slept badly and he had a neck thick as the trunk of a redwood tree. And underneath ... how could anything be that big? It was like some awful dangling Chinese lantern. Shelley looked away from it, only to catch sight of Matthew Harvey in the farmhouse doorway, and her face burned.

'Oh yes,' said Shelley, on her guard. 'It's very peaceful. Except for my brother of course.'

She'd left Adam swinging on the five-bar metal gate, chattering with Billy Harvey, who looked to be about his age, fifteen. Going on three, in Adam's case.

Mrs Harvey was picking feathers and wisps of hay from the eggs. 'Sometimes there are funny noises in that cottage,' she said. 'I – er – but it's been all right, has it?' She gave Shelley a quick glance, then looked back to the eggs.

I could almost tell her, thought Shelley, and then resisted the temptation. 'I don't hear anyone, if that's what you mean,' she said. 'Just the wind and the sheep. Oh, and the water.'

'Water? Can you hear that from the cottage? Course I wouldn't know, that reservoir's not been there that many years. We lived in the cottage when we first got married. Frank said it was to be mine, it was a young wife's house, but I never liked it, I never settled. He couldn't get the old girl at the farm to go to the cottage. She wasn't going to give up this farmhouse to me, oh no! Then she died.'

Shelley saw that Mrs Harvey had the same gleaming dark eyes as Matthew. She had tried to tame her hair, so that over her head rippled waves round and tight as sausages. She must set her hair in curlers.

'The old girl – was that your mother-in-law?'

'Yes. After she died we moved up here. More work, mind, all that plaster moulding to clean, all those cornices and flowers on the ceiling. Cobwebs and soot caught there. And I used to hear the old girl sweeping up the yard, long after she'd gone. Again and again.

18

Sweeping. Making me feel a right slattern.' She turned away. At the back, her hair, dark as molasses, was threaded with silver. 'Sometimes I still hear her,' she said, and walked out across the yard.

Oh, do you, thought Shelley. Well, no comment. I wonder when Joan was there . . . She called, 'Which was built first, Mrs Harvey, the cottage or the farm?'

'The cottage. Middle of the eighteenth. Seventeen sixties, I think. Then the farm was built a little later, by William Harvey and his three sons. You can see over the door, look. 1779. We've always let the cottage, never sold it. I don't know if Matt'll want to live there when he comes back from college.'

College?

In the doorway Matthew folded his arms and grinned. Shelley saw that he was wearing a white cotton shirt with a granddad collar, not his farm worker's blue Babygro.

'Don't know if Matt'll what?' he said.

'We're just talking about End Cottage, Matt.'

He said, 'I don't see myself in that dinky little house, Mum. Not the way you've got it done.' He winked at Shelley, a quick eclipse of the jet of his eye. She flinched. He could not even pretend to be shy out of politeness. He was so confident here, wasn't he? On his big farm with its acid smell of cow-muck and its tractors with their wheels high as her face, and that bull with its enormous plonker like a nightmare hose-pipe . . . there must be something wrong with it.

'She says she hears the water,' Mrs Harvey said to Matthew. 'All that way.'

'Do you?' he said, staring. 'Funny how sound travels.'

'They should never have built it,' said Mrs Harvey, a little tremor in her voice. 'It disturbs everything. The land's not a house to be knocked down and rebuilt. But you don't hear much else?'

Does she want me to say Yes or No, wondered Shelley. She shook her head.

'There's a lot to see round here, you know,' said Matthew, taking over. His mother seemed to fade willingly alongside him. 'There's great views across the countryside. And it's walking country. You can go for walks over the hilltops. Watch out for the mines, though.'

'Mines?'

'Old lead mines. Even the Romans mined round here. Or their slaves did. What are you doing tomorrow? Shelley, isn't it? Wild and poetical, sounds about right for you. I only know your name because your brother told our Billy. I'll call for you about eleven, shall I?'

'Oh. All right. Yes,' said Shelley, taken aback, thinking, I wonder what else Dogbreath told them about me?

Adam barged in between them, cried, 'Have you heard their budgie, Shell? It's got a Derbyshire accent. It goes, "Hey oop me duck."'

He's like Charlie Chaplin, she thought, jerky walk in those loose jeans and the deliberately baggy wool jumper. Utterly easy. Utterly irritating.

She said quickly, 'What are you studying, Matthew?'

'Physics,' he said.

'What!' screamed Adam. 'You're never a physicist! You look normal!'

Matthew grinned. 'Physics and maths and multiverses. These are a few of my favourite things.'

'God!' cried Adam. 'Or perhaps it should be, definitely not God? I watched a study programme about quantum physics, all multiverses and parallel worlds and time an illusion. No linear time, all that stuff, I tell you, they were barking!'

'Who?' said Matthew.

'The physicists, or whatever they were. Man, were they mad! One looked just like a pelican and he lived in the middle of a great nest of books. The other was bald as an egg and he was going on about *"all time is present!"* Weird, eyes like a frog.' Adam pulled a face like a wide-mouthed frog and somehow his eyes bulged, and they all laughed.

'We must go, Adam,' Shelley said.

Mrs Harvey edged round her son. 'I've washed the eggs,' she said. 'You're lucky. Sometimes we get short at this time of year, but there's a few come into lay since Christmas.'

'We just shout "Battery!" and they drop one straight away,' said Matthew, smiling at her.

'Hey!' cried Adam. 'We're going to the water soon. Do you want to come, Billy?'

'All right!' cried Billy. 'I'll just sort the heifers and I'll be down.'

Great, thought Shelley. Mum and Dave, Billy and Adam. And me.

Well, I'm certainly not inviting Matthew, but as if to answer her he said, 'I've got Far Oldfield to do today. I'll go and change.'

It always came back to Shelley by herself. She had felt her solitude acutely that morning, woken by the soft sounds of her mother and Dave making love, trying to be quiet, so that she would not hear in her little room so close to theirs. So that she would not intrude upon their togetherness. So that she would not be there with them. So that they would keep her out of their love. Such faint, furtive sounds she knew instinctively what they were doing.

Her mother making love with Dave; Dave the engineer, the koala bear with the bald patch and the round nose and the man-made fibre jumper with the diamond patterns in grey and red. Sometimes he pushed out his jumper with his fists, but this was the most aggressive movement he made. Dave was uncaring of the way he looked. Just as well really. He stomped through the world sloping slightly forward from his waist, or from where his waist might have been under the misshapen jumper. She couldn't think what colour his eyes were behind his once trendy green-rimmed specs, but they were usually blinking at her mother. He had a placid smile, enough money for them to live on and two well-adjusted grown-up sons who did everything right, and slightly disapproved of their father 'living in sin'.

Now he had Adam, too, in case he got withdrawal symptoms because his own sons were grown-up. Adam would never be a surveyor or an economics student like them. No. He'd either be Superclown or the first crook to turn crime into a performance art.

Some entrepreneur into private health care for the terminally mad could employ Adam to push people right off their rockers and send profits hurtling sky-high. Adam the Appalling. Adam the Abysmal One.

It was still dark when she'd woken. Shelley had eased herself out of bed. She had her books downstairs, waiting for her, full of promises. She would sit in the kitchen and drink tea. She wouldn't hear their love down there. She crept downstairs, forgetting, and Joan's voice started up again.

'Ere! Will yer listen? I don't want to sit by misen, I'm cowd, I want to be in the 'ouse with smoke potherin' and summat fryin', a bit of fat lambkin, but I mun hide.

Is it Childermas agin? Unluckiest day of the year, it is. It was for me . . .

Let me tell yer 'ow it started goin' bad. Me fayther brought his new wife here. And a right ditherin' poor thing she was. She's soft in th'ead and she thinks I'm called Addie! I tell 'er, "I'm Joan Harvey, not yer Addie. They say you lost yer daughter Addie, years ago. And my mother, she died, I never knew 'er!"

She 'as great wild eyes, this new wife. Like a hare. And when she's mezzled she calls me Addie and flaps her hands around like a bird that's bin hurt.

They're building a big farm up at top. They won't tek me with 'em. The new wife brung napkins and a table cloth and a squab. And 'er son. She speaks so dainty. They came from Buxton way, yer see, poor as mice, but thought they was above us all, because her fost man was schooled. So was the son. They was too good for us then! Her fost man was set on that mine. Now it's ours. Fayther says there's rich veins of lead there.

They won't let me there. "Don't you go near that mine, Joanie, don't you! On pain of death!" That was both on 'em. Now why? I'm used to workin' at a minehead, knockin' and washin' and sortin' the ore. But not this mine, Joanie. It's summat special! Too special for you.

I'm cowd. Stuck. I'm stuck here, Fat Joan with the stone at me back. They say I'm obstreperous, they say I'm addled, they say I mekk up stories, but I don't, I never. I'll tell you why I'm stuck here, if you'll only listen then –

'No, I've heard enough!' cried Shelley. 'I know you're going to tell me why you're stuck with the stone at your back, Joan, but not this morning. I've got a bad feeling about it.'

Shelley ran into the kitchen and shut the door fast, fixed the latch firm against Fat Joanie with all her muttered incantations.

Four

Across the water skimmed a yacht, swift as a dragonfly. Shelley watched it dart and curve in towards the pale shore. Its sail was a perfect wing of blue. The fair-headed yachtsman stood tall, as if he grew out of his craft, like a figurehead.

'Arion with the dolphins,' mused Shelley.

The blue-sailed yacht was the only boat on the water this afternoon. The others were moored up on the pebbles, their tall masts tinkling in the wind, like bells high in thin steeples. Around one bobbed a man in a Popeye cap, while his wife shivered in her mauve shell-suit. Otherwise the shore was deserted.

Shelley knew it had once all been water, millions of years ago, warm oceans with small islands and lagoons. Just imagine it. Cold, dank Derbyshire under tropical seas, with coral reefs, underwater forests of sea lillies where molluscs and soft-footed brachiopods hid. When the waters at last drew back, some things survived from the slime and grew legs or wings, but those creatures' little bodies were trapped in a vast upland, stranded forever in the great limestone sweeps. Shelley remembered a primary school outing when they searched for the little fossilised remains.

Now this water stretched away, spreading silver fingers towards the distant hills. It was too wide to be natural, a valley spread too far. It looked like a sea of silver foil, the thin foil that wrapped those little chocolate rolls Adam stuffed whole into his mouth, foil you can wrinkle with your fingers. The landscape was ordered, altered, with dark conifers planted in neat forests on the far hills, a place designed, considered and planned.

Her father, Declan, could have painted this lake and its hills in watercolour, mixing purples and blues and browns and greys so that the colours ran together and could not be named. He loved those colours. In her mind he wore a jumper hand-knitted in earth colours, russet and peat with a tree of life pattern knitted in the stitching. He wouldn't be seen dead in acrylic diamonds like Dave.

Shelley followed Dave and her mother and Adam and Billy around the courtyard bordered by gift shops and what Mum called a Naff Caff. The shops were full of plastic pencil ends, and scented candles and floral tins full of comfits, all the things you never knew you wanted, even after you'd bought them.

'I want an ice cream and I want it now,' screamed Adam in a baby voice so that Billy shrieked with laughter. A woman scrabbled in a freezer, warning Adam first that, 'The ice cream season is over, duck.'

'Not for me,' cried Adam.

The two boys capered away along the waterside path, waving their ice creams defiantly at the sleet which had just begun to fall. It was cold here, even colder than in the village.

Shelley watched her mum and Dave covertly. Her mother wore a cherry-red jacket and black leggings. She'd lost weight recently, perhaps because she didn't sit up late at night any more stuffing her face with Thorntons chocolate misshapes. She always left the lemon creams for Shelley and the praline for Adam, no matter how drunk she was.

For years strings of dull orange scarecrow's hair had hidden her mother's face. Shelley's hair was the same colour, but not so harsh. 'Like shiny new coins,' her mother told her, reaching out a hand to touch the curls so that Shelley flinched away. Now Mum had her hair cut into a bell shape, and she looked good, Shelley had to admit that. She had seen her father's new wife, Mo, when she was pregnant. Mo looked so huge, in her silky, purple, Indian dress, like an air balloon just beginning to deflate in a field. Shelley pictured her as a female toad with Dad clinging to her back.

It must be Mo who didn't want her for Christmas. Let it be Mo, prayed Shelley. And yet when Shelley had visited them, she'd tried so hard with her half-brother and half-sister, she'd made them a chocolate cake, she'd let them scramble over her and yank her long plait until the tears came to her eyes. They had watched her build them palaces from Duplo and then ripped them apart with caws of triumph. Shelley did not like little children, they had everything far too near the surface, but she had tried.

Surely Dad could not still think she was strange in the head? She had never mentioned hearing things again. The very last time was when she'd heard the stonemason's boy scream as he fell from the vaulting in the cathedral, amid the murmurings from the stone heads of kings and saints and cherubs and the odd demon spying on the tourists. Voices chanted and murmured in the high stone vaulting as if birds wheeled in shoals.

Oh, and then there was the voice of a boy, pleading for the life of his blind sister, pleading for her not to be burned . . . that was in a street in Derby. Dad was cross when she told him, but, after all, it was partly his fault the voices had started seeking her out. One of the first times she remembered hearing voices was when she had run back into infant school to fetch the Russian dolls he had given her for her birthday. They stood on the display table. The dolls lived one inside the other. They were made of painted wood, bright yellow, red and blue under shining varnish. You could set them out and knock them down like dominoes. Her mother was furious that she liked them so.

At home time Shelley had wanted the dolls and ran back into school to take them home. And then she'd heard voices. Children singing *Sally go round the Sun*, high beyond the beams in the lofty, empty, Victorian classroom.

At least she'd left Joan by the cottage stairs. There was just her own family here. There they were now. Not much of a family for her. Adam, light, bright Adam and his friend, and Mum and Dave with their soft, flushed faces.

'No one for me,' she said. 'Nothing of mine.' She turned away from them and hurried along the path, past a pair of swans who sat with softly-raised wings in the shallows, past a middle-aged woman scuttling behind a small Cairn with a poop scoop at the ready, past couples and families. She followed the path round one side of the water towards a little hill.

The path wound helter-skelter style up the hill and between tall upright stones. They were not old standing stones, not a circle of worship or meeting, but a sculptor's arrangement of gritstone pillars. The gritstones were different heights, placed at intervals, and they each had toeholes for children and a hole at eye-level. You could peep through at the little villages in the surrounding hills, at farms and churches and rocks. You could even see the miner's hill. That wasn't planned. It was picked at, hacked at and finally spent. The holes were like view finders, or picture frames, made for an onlooker, an outsider like herself.

She spied on them, Mum and Dave and the two boys, from behind her stone. It was magical, like being in another world. She remembered reading that the Celts thought you could cure a sick baby by passing it through a hole in a stone. You could join hands with someone through such a stone and pledge yourself in betrothal. The Celts saw inner and outer worlds, like the world between a tree and its bark. Stones lived, they leaped from the secret world in the centre of the earth.

She wandered up to the stone at the highest point of the hill and gazed through. Suddenly it darkened. For a split second she thought it was her father, watching her.

'Boo!' said someone.

Shelley's heart jumped against her ribs. She stepped back and peered round the stone.

The man wasn't at all like her father, except for his height. He was much younger. He must be in his twenties. His hair was pale as the moon, cut long and silky on the top, shaved at the sides.

'Sorry I scared you,' he said. 'I couldn't resist it. I saw you from my yacht earlier, I think.'

'Yes, I saw you on the yacht with the dragonfly sail,' she said.

'That's a nice description,' he said.

His eyes were blue and clear. She had to look away, so she spied on the others. They were wandering around on the far shore looking pathetic. They were wondering where she was. Her mother was making silly little runs up and down the lakeside, like some red-coated water bird searching for her brood, not knowing what to do with her hands. As if I'm three, thought Shelley gleefully. Little does she know I'm here, with a delicious guy.

'Well, I must go,' he said, glancing over his shoulder. 'Be seeing you.'

She watched him striding away, straight-backed, in trainers white as snow. TOO FAST TO RACE was emblazoned in white on his black sweatshirt, above the design of a yacht listing with the wind. She watched him all the way to the car park, tried to tell the make of his car. Maybe a Porsche, that shape, she thought. It whizzed away fast, whatever it was. She stood on the hill, not wanting to move, not wanting the intrusion of the others. She didn't want to see her mother's face light up and that mock jaunty wave. Quick, turn away.

Shelley hurried along the edge of the water, then headed up a bank of thick tussocked grass. She saw it just in time before she would have crushed it with her foot and killed it.

She was too fearful to look closely at first. It was soft, rounded, grey-brown. It might be a rat. There might be blood. When they'd driven up the road to the village after Christmas there was a squashed rabbit on the road. 'Tomato puree squiggles!' Adam had squealed.

There was no naked rat's tail, and it wasn't a rabbit; it had speckled feathers, and a sad little crest. Its beak was open, gasping. Soundless. She touched the soft feathers with light fingers, felt the tiny panic of its heart.

She stood up. The wind was cold now, sleet slanted against her face, while cries and calls from the land and water circled round her head. If she left the bird there it would die. Someone would tread on it, or a dog would devour it, or some wild creature would steal it away in the night. It would freeze, small beak forever open soundlessly in death.

But she didn't like birds. They fluttered and beat their wings and pecked and scratched with their long toes. They didn't belong down here, they wanted their freedom.

She knelt down and slipped her hands around its warm lightness, little cage of bone, terrified that she might crush and splinter its wings. It was too weak to struggle. She saw a tremor in its throat, fragile as a speckled egg. Its beak opened helplessly and it made a faint sound, a chirrup.

Shelley sighed. She didn't want it, but how could she desert it? Now she did need to find them, and get home with the poor bird.

Her mother was trotting along the path, mouth open stupidly, still searching for her. The moment she saw Shelley she teetered to a walk and smiled nonchalantly. 'Ready to go, darling? We're all cold,' she cried. 'Oh! What have you got there? A bird?'

'Right first time, Mother. It'll die if I leave it.'

On the way back to the village in Dave's car, they passed a tractor in a field. 'It's our Matthew,' Billy told them. Matthew sat high in the cab, watching a group of piebald beasts with long, pointed horns, like the horns of Highland cattle. He might have seen the car but did not wave. A cloud of birds waited on the wind behind the tractor.

Matthew will know about the bird, thought Shelley.

Five

'It'll be a skylark,' said Matthew.

'Oh, I don't think so, it's quite ordinary,' she said.

'Has it got a crest?'

'Well, almost. Just a tuft really.'

'And you say it's speckled?'

'Yes. Sort of drab speckles. It's not small. I mean, it's not like a wren, or even a robin.'

'It's a skylark!' he insisted. 'Don't you know skylarks? You should hear them above the pasture in the spring. They're mostly too high to see, mind. The song is beautiful. It's endless, like liquid silver. As if it's poured high between two cups.'

Shelley stared at him in amazement.

'It eats insects,' he said gruffly. 'And it'll die.'

'And it may not,' she retorted. 'I'm keeping it warm in my room. And I've used a medicine dropper to feed it.'

'What with?'

'Ready Brek,' she admitted. 'It's all I could think of.'

'Ah. Who'd have thought you'd be so soppy, Shelley Taylor?'

Reluctantly, she was out with him that morning, at the cable car terminus. She turned away from Matthew, ready for the ride. If she had to spend time with someone, get it over with quickly. Three tiny bubbles hung high on cables as fine as silk, as if a spider had swung from one side of the gorge all the way across to the other.

'Are those the cable cars?' she said, almost laughing in disbelief.

'That's them,' said Matthew.

Shelley had tried to pay the four pounds for her ticket at the office, so as not to be in any way beholden to him, but 'No,' he had said, closing her hand over her money. 'I asked you. I'll pay.' You're so old-fashioned, she thought, I suppose you keep the women in their place down on the farm.

'You can pay for a drink later,' he said.

Now they waited in silence. The cable cars swung in to the terminus, and slowed down, pursuing their horseshoe-shaped groove in the ground. They didn't look much larger than they had when they were suspended between the cliffs.

Matthew took her hand. His hand was so warm. With a shock she saw that the two middle fingers stopped below the knuckles or where the knuckles should have been. They were just stumps. Well, it's his left hand so I suppose it's not as bad as it could be, she thought, too startled to take her hand back. She tried not to move her head as she looked. It was certainly odd, but it wasn't as revolting as she might have thought.

'The door hasn't closed,' she hissed.

'It's all right, it will,' he said. At last it did, curving to complete the bubble and seal them in, as they slid out of the terminus and lurched into nothing.

'I shouldn't have come,' said Shelley.

'Of course you should,' he murmured. But he didn't realise, did he? This little goldfish bowl could never hold them up! There wasn't enough oxygen for more than a few minutes, there was no air vent, they were too heavy, the car was too fragile.

'Hey, Shelley, look down,' cried Matthew. 'See that dark speck down in the car park? That's the Land-Rover!'

'Sit still,' cried Shelley, sure that the car was rocking wildly. She would be sick. Where? There was no window to open, no room to throw up on the floor without it splashing up his legs. No. It was worse than that, she was going to lose control, completely and utterly, go berserk, beat the windows, scrabble at the doors, burst the bubble and jump out into nothingness. She could not breathe. She was drenched in sweat. It was like being buried in the sky, and there was crying in her head, but it wasn't Joan this time. It was her own cries. She shut her lips tight. Nothing must escape from them, no word, no sound, or she would disintegrate and float in pieces across that void.

The cable car stopped. They were hanging in the middle of the gorge. This was where she had first seen the cable cars. Don't look, down or up or out, don't look anywhere. It was swaying, wasn't it? It was going to fall off the cable.

She felt a hand burning her shoulder. It would leave a strange brand mark, a hand minus two fingers.

Matthew leant lightly against her. She had no resistance. 'It's all right,' he said softly. 'They wait here a while for people to take photographs. It's all right. You can look, you know.'

After an age she opened her eyes, first like slits, so that nothing dreadful could slip in. She saw trees growing sideways from the cliffs, and a bird circling below them where it ought not to be.

'It's all right, Shelley,' he said again, that soft voice soothing her. 'It's not really high. You know, your skylark would be higher than this.'

'I wish it would begin,' she whispered, and it did. The vibration jarred her taut body. The car lurched forward and they were off again.

At last she knew by some sense that there was a surface not far below them. The car shook. The side gaped open.

Shelley fell through it, pushed her feet down on to the earth, felt her body rooted just where it should be, not over the earth, or under it, but on it. She turned to Matthew and smiled.

'Are you all right now?' he asked. 'I'm sorry. I didn't realise it would scare you.'

'Neither did I,' she admitted. 'I'm sorry too. I just got the feeling that something dreadful was going to happen.'

'And it didn't.'

'No it didn't,' she said. 'Not today.'

'Sort of déjà vu, was it?' he said. 'Sort of, pretentious *moi*?'

She laughed, then said, 'Yes. I don't like being shut in.'

'Then don't fall down a mine. You won't like it,' he teased. 'Let's have a coffee.'

She couldn't take her eyes off his hand as they sat at a rather damp picnic table outside with their coffees and apricot Danish pastries.

'It isn't that bad is it?' he said and she blushed, said, 'I'm sorry, I shouldn't stare. I – I just wondered . . .'

'You wondered what happened? Good. I hate people pretending not to notice I've got eight and two halves. I caught it in a baling machine when I was a lad, that's all.'

'That's all?'

He shrugged. 'Could have been all of them.'

'I bet your mother felt terrible when it happened.'

'She did. She wanted to take me to the infirmary but I insisted on having my dinner first, because it was egg and chips. Then the doctor was mad 'cos I'd eaten. She gave my dad hell for not having watched me all the time, but how could he?'

'I don't think I've seen your dad,' said Shelley.

Matthew shrugged. 'He's out in the fields a lot,' he said. 'And I'm the eldest son of the eldest son, and I'm getting out of farming. So we have our disagreements. Billy'll take over, it's his life. Now then, Shelley, while we're on dads, that's not your dad at the cottage, is it?'

'How can you tell?'

''Cos he's a different shape, he's Mr Blobby to your Olive Oil. And he was so polite to you when we left the cottage this morning.

Real dads aren't that polite. What does he do?'

'He's an engineer. In a car factory. Sort of management engineer.'

'Looks like one. What does your own dad do then?'

'He works for a company that makes paints and pastels and papers. He paints too, he's good.' She pushed her finger into the soft apricot in the centre of her pastry. 'He's different from Mum and podgy Dave. And I'm like him. I'm not like them.'

'Do you know what, Shelley?' Matthew leaned forward and his eyes gleamed dark as peat water. 'I think . . . I think you are going to give your mum and her man a hard time.'

'Oh *do* you?' she cried. 'Well, it's not your business! It's *me* who has the hard time. It's all right for people like you, you're part of a real conventional family, part of a big set-up, aren't you? I'm not. Can you think how that feels? You've got your father. My father doesn't . . . you've got both your father and mother and you live where your family has lived for hundreds of years.' She wrenched the Danish pastry into two so that flakes of sugar icing flew off all around the little table.

'Actually, it's a drag sometimes,' he said. 'You've no idea what daft feuds there can be in a little village like ours. Families turn their faces away, cross the street, kids beat each other up in the playground. All because of who nicked a lead mine from whom in 1689 or who was Barmaster for the local mines and ruled against your great-great-great whatever in 1800, who stole a pig from whom in 1835, who got whom pregnant in 1932, and who flogged whom a duff motor . . . and stop bullying that pastry.'

She smiled, she couldn't help it. Then she said, 'Matthew, what did your mother mean the other morning at the farm – had I heard anything?'

He frowned as if he didn't understand. Shelley went on, 'She kept asking me if I'd heard anything. I don't know what she meant,' she lied.

He groaned. 'My mother... She's got a thing about – well, ghosts, I suppose. She doesn't see them, but she hears them, hears them all over the place. She walks in a wood a few miles away from here when the bluebells and wood anemones are out. She says she knows there's a ghost woman sits and knits there, because she can hear the needles click and even the roughness of the wool rubbing together.'

'Does she hear ghosts in your farmhouse?'

'Yes, she says folks laugh and chase each other round what's now our bathroom. But the cottage is different. Serious. I suppose I shouldn't say that to you really, as you're staying there. But Mum thinks there was family bother, way way back in the past. Some girl shut in somewhere.'

Stuck here, Fat Joan with the stone at me back...
Shelley felt as if a cold hand had encircled the back of her neck.

Matthew shrugged, then gave an unexpectedly tender smile. 'She's very soft-hearted, my Mum. She'd listen to anyone with a problem. Even a problem from the past.' He raised his eyes and looked at Shelley.

'Do you believe her?' she asked nervously.

'In a way. I think the past is hanging around for those who want it. I don't want to know all the nasty bits, thank you. We can't do owt about it now.'

'What does your dad say?'

'He says it's the menopause.'

'How patronising!' cried Shelley.

'I can be much more patronising than *that*,' he leered, leaning forward and tucking a strand of hair behind Shelley's ear. 'Women open themselves more to hurt, that's all. Look at you! Don't take everything so hard! Go with the flow.'

'Thank you, Agony Auntie Harvey,' she said, thinking that she should feel crosser than this.

'Any time. Come on,' he said. 'Don't step on the birds.' Flurries of sparrows had converged on the pastry crumbs.

Shelley had not travelled in a Land-Rover before. It was a new one, but the floor mats were grooved with mud and there were balls of crumpled chocolate foil and Bounty wrappers all over. She frowned at an enormous syringe.

'Sheep wormer, not heroin,' said Matthew.

She could see everything from the high cab, the hills just peaking away from them, the higgledy-piggledy walls of choppy yellow-grey stone.

'I guess the reservoir has made a difference to your lives,' she said.

'Yeah. Tourists. Caravans crawling round our lanes, nose to tail like elephants,' he grumbled. 'Bed and breakfast with supermarket croissants. Prosperity for some, sure, but it all feels different round here now. The village had been closed off to the world for centuries, especially in the winter. No reason for people to come here. Now anyone can, and does. And there's money coming in, money to buy up workers' cottages and twee them up. Barn conversions.'

'What about your parents?'

'I think they resented the valley being flooded. They knew farmers who farmed there years ago, that kind of thing. Not that the land was much cop, but there's been the noise and the construction traffic. And then those men who were killed in a landslide. Four workers. Young men. Something gave way and they were covered by a fall of mud.'

'How horrible,' whispered Shelley.

'Yes,' said Matthew. 'The land is always here. We're not.'

They drove back to the village. Matthew pulled in by the stile further down the street. 'Come on,' he said. 'Let's walk.'

They climbed through the stone wall, into a flock of shrieking geese, their wild blue eyes ringed with orange. Matthew drove them off the track. They were in narrow strip fields, poor pasture, as if the hillside wore a hairshirt of scrub and scratchy hawthorn. Here and there were tiny oases of thyme, vetch and scabious, blackened by winter frost and rain.

The hill was pockmarked with the shafts and dips of old mines. Matthew pointed them out to her, murmuring their names like an incantation: Perseverance, Horse Buttocks, Cursed Moor, Poor Man's

Venture, Swallow's Nest, Nickalum. The shafts were strengthened by girders and concrete slabs, and the openings barred by old railway sleepers, barbed wire, wooden pallets.

I hate it, thought Shelley as she stumbled up the hill. The mines were like bumps in the land, termites' burrows. One was quite open, round, its stones set like a well with bright ferns between them.

'You must lose a lot of sheep and lambs here,' she said.

'Not many,' he said. 'It's great here in spring. There's celandines and cowslips, and skylarks flitting and singing up with the spirits in the heavens, like yours will when she's better. So high they're in another world. You look as if you don't believe me.'

'It's hard to believe,' said Shelley. The higher they climbed, the more she could see rocky outcrops as if splinters of the earth's bones were sticking out.

'Rocks over there remind me of a cathedral,' said Matthew.

'I think they were there long before there were cathedrals,' said Shelley darkly.

'I'm sure they were. Nearly at the top of the pasture now,' he said.

Some pasture, thought Shelley sourly. The word suggested softness and nurturing to her, and there was nothing nurturing about this place. It was barren and exhausted.

'The mine up there was worked by my family for a long while,' said Matthew. 'The stones left are from the coe where the miner got ready for work, kept his hat and candles and such.'

'And what's it called?' she asked.

'Harvey's Rake. It was called Addie's Fortune before that, I believe.'

'Addie?' Shelley said, trying to remember something, trying to hear, wanting to know in spite of herself. 'Why was it Addie's Fortune?'

'I'm not sure. Some girl, by the sound of it. In the 1760s or 1770s. Miner's girlfriend, or missus, I suppose. No, I think it was his daughter.'

Daughter who wasn't there, Shelley suddenly realised. Joan had gabbled on about her father's new wife bringing her son with her. She hadn't said the daughter was there. Shelley shivered.

'Have my jacket,' Matthew said, putting it over her shoulders before she could stop him. 'It's going to snow, I bet. Fifty pence for who spots the first flaw.'

Shelley climbed up the last rough steps and sat down by the mine. She needed the emptiness, the space here. It suited her just now.

'Hey, shut down time again, is it?' teased Matthew. 'Do you want to go for a drink?'

'No,' she said.

'You're a hard one to reach,' he said, quietly, not offended by her refusal. 'Hey well, I'd better get up that field for a while, check out those ewes. I'll be a little while. I like to put a bit of work in for them while I'm at home. Be careful now, Shelley Taylor.'

'Here! Take your coat,' she called.

'Keep it, mardy girl,' he said, and he ran down the hill without looking back at her.

It was good to sit up here, apart.

She sifted the smaller stones in the pile around the mine shaft, easing them between her fingers. Behind her was the black crest of the trees she had seen from her window, the Mohican's hair on this skull of a hill. Below her was the village. Shelley wondered if they were at home in the cottage with the stinking stairwell, and the damp. This morning as she stood outside the cottage she had noticed a wavering tower of stones, where the constant fires had destroyed the chimney cement and caused them to be repointed. Yet all those fires had never conquered the damp. Adam would run out of incense soon, they wouldn't sell incense in the village stores. Adam! The bane of her life, and the love of her mother's. Her mother loved Adam passionately, idiotically, almost as much as she must have loved Dad and now loved Dave. She teased Adam, flirted with him, was amused and cajoled by him.

Her dad was so different from Dave. No owlish stare there. Her dad was lean and witty, creative . . . Yet something was not clear. Why wouldn't it come clear?

Her mother would be in the cottage now, chopping leeks and potatoes for home-made soup, trilling and humming little scales in time to her knife. She was happy. Perhaps Shelley just got in her way.

Shelley looked at the stones in her hand. Something glinted.

Carefully she picked it out. It was a piece of glass, weathered and dulled, shaped like a butterfly's wing.

She polished it on Matthew's jacket and held it up before her face. It was flowing with waves of purple, yellow and white. In one area the waves of strong colour converged so that the light was not let in. The crystal thickened into dark blood red, and then the waves flowed away into the shallower colours, pale purple, saffron and cream, delicate as crocus flowers.

'I know this, it's Blue John crystal,' she whispered. 'They sell it in all the gift shops.' She turned it over and over in her hand.

Down in the village a cockerel crowed. A sheepdog barked and leaped to the end of its chain as a horse forged up the street. Its flanks were glossy as newly-peeled chestnuts and the rider sat straight in hard hat, jacket and high boots. There was money now in this old mining village, money for Range Rovers and thoroughbred horses, money to put leaded-light windows and superstore doors in the small homes of hardship. The middle classes put up extensions, leylandii, and wattle fences, desperate for privacy where before closeness had been necessary to survival.

Today the winter sun was just a fleeting visitor. For a moment its slanting light skewered the insubstantial cluster of cottages around the squat grey church. The first few snowflakes drifted out of the leaden sky and floated around Shelley's face as she sat by the mine, arms wrapped around her knees, waiting.

'I know someone's there,' she said. 'I'm too tired to move. Go on then, I'm listening. Is it Joan? Are you going to tell me more about your dad's new wife and her son . . . it all sounds familiar. I could do with *my* family sorting out!'

Joan was silent.

Six

It wasn't Joan's gabble, not here. Joan had always sounded confused, like an angry child. This voice was sweeter, softer, and so much fainter Shelley thought it must come from further back in time.

My name is Addie, Addie Johnson. Can you hear my voice among so many?

The hillside seethes with voices. They whirl like wraiths through the mines, under stones and tumbledowns. They drift under water in the drowned valley. They wind in and out of crumbled beast shelters. They are all waiting for their listeners. They have stories to tell, in wisps and threads, and often their stories have no endings. Hear them. Catch them if you can.

I am a prisoner here. I want to be released by love.

In the last hours of my freedom I had gone to Crow Wood. A witchball sun hung low in the midwinter sky, with a promise of another day. I was alone, while my mother and my brother, Hugh, huddled together over the little fire in the house, the fire that I had made, that hissed and spat around logs green-skinned as dragons.

My mother fastens to Hugh like old man's beard to the hedgerow. Perhaps she does not love me because of my disfigurement? My skin is pocked and pitted so that I hide my face. I caught the cowpox from my sweet Celandine, you see, I tended her, no one else would do it.

I had gone to Crow Wood to fetch holly. The berries would bring a notion of warmth to our house, they show us life everlasting, they keep away witches. My little dog Jack wheeled joyfully about me, now and then dipping his nose in the snow. Nearby, a robin redbreast danced on twig-like legs to cheer me by his splash of scarlet on the white.

All day the dark had glistened in the hollows and soon the world began to dim though it was but three o'clock.

When I came back home that December afternoon, I saw my father's pick lying by the door, the pick he had used to cut lead from this very mine. All around, the snow was pockmarked by drops. The drops were red.

I saw the little lamb there too, running about for its mother, bleating. Out came my brother Hugh and smote it, so that the blood spurted from it and its small bleating died away. My brother stole the sheep. It was a theve. Worse, it was William Harvey's theve. William Harvey is a man of turbulent temper, and as a theve is young she would give many more lambs. My brother is a fool!

I opened our house door. The thick stink of rich flesh made my stomach heave, used as it was lately only to bland oat bread and porridge. There stood my mother and brother, close together, wearing complicity like a cloak.

'Do not be frightened, Addie,' wheedled my brother. 'I have hid the bones up on Worm Edge. The lamb I shall attend to shortly. There will be more snow to cover the signs. We have to eat somehow, Sister! I will not be a pauper, reliant on the parish, wandering from village to village for all to point at.'

'You will ruin us, you fool!' I hissed.

'See what a wasp your daughter is become, Mother?' he sneered. 'Her tongue is crabbed, her face too, like an apple the worms have eaten! Addie Johnson, a bitter old maid before her time. No man will ever want her. She will bring no son to keep you in your later years!'

'They will come after you for this,' I cried. 'William Harvey and his sons will take revenge. He will fetch the constables, and them from the village that despise us, and they will all band together. They will put you before the Justices for this felony, Hugh. They hate us, they say we think ourselves above them, they say we scorn them.' I turned on my mother. 'William Harvey always wanted you for himself. Father told me. Harvey hated Father coming down from Buxton. He thought you would be his, thought Father stole you from him.'

She turned away her great eyes and whispered, 'That was a long time ago, and William married first.'

'But now he has no wife. She died bearing their last child.'

'The idiot daughter, Joan,' sneered Hugh.

'William Harvey will have you and the mine, Mother,' I cried. 'He will put Hugh before the Justice. And will the Justice care that we starve? Never! He'll send Hugh to the gallows!'

At that my mother started up and cried, 'No! I could not bear it!'

Hugh was her first child. My mother had borne him when she was barely fifteen years of age. She had been with child twice more but had lost them to the heaviness of the ore she worked with at the minehead. Another child died from too much soporific for his cough when he was two, and my father told me they had no money for the headstones for these little ones, though my mother tried to beg them from the mason.

Last she had borne me, and I was not favourite. In her eyes, Hugh could do no wrong. Sometimes it seemed to me that their closeness had in some manner hastened my father's death. My father died a month ago. He had the miner's disease of the chest, coughing and without breath, and his body was poisoned by the very lead he sought. My father turned his face away from them and died in pain and sadness.

My mother did not care. She would miss Hugh more, it seemed. 'They cannot take my son,' she cried. 'I could not watch you dragged from me to be hanged.' And over and over she twisted her hands.

Hugh looked sideways at me. 'I should make my escape soon, in the dark,' he said, but she begged, 'No!' and clung to his sleeve. He dragged her like a broken-winged bird and tried to loose her fingers one by one so that I thought he would break them.

And I cried, 'Wait!'

My mother and my brother turn to look at me. Firelight flickers in their eyes. Silence hangs thick as woodsmoke. I cannot bear her weakness. Her eyes are soft as water, soft like the eyes of my Celandine. She sold Celandine, and her calf. She killed my hens. She never sees my endeavour, baking bread, growing salats in the garth, sweeping and strewing our house with sweet-smelling hay and rushes, she never pays heed, only to him. He steals all her affection.

And the more she flings me from her, the more I want her love! I remember the mother who rocked me when the wind pulled at our house. She told me tales of the great dragon who lay under Wormhill and breathed sheets of fire into the storm. I was warm, safe then in her arms. If I go in Hugh's place, and take the blame, she will love me again.

I said, 'Wait!'

Hugh's face was set hard as an axe, but he let me speak.

'William will bring down his flock from the uplands to shelter from this snow. He will find the theve and her lamb are gone, and come to hammer on this door. Tell him I ran away, you know not where or why.'

They still did not speak, either of them.

'For a while the Harveys may think I am the felon, not you, Brother. They will not find me, they will forget me and blame the jaggers. The jaggers are here to take the wool, I heard their bells.'

'You are right,' says Hugh. 'They are in the alehouse. They cannot drive their ponies over the peak in this deep snow.'

She watched my face, her great eyes hungry.

'I will hide up in the mine. And when it is all safe, Mother, come for me. I will wait for you to come.'

She is still, then flies to fetch a keeping-pot of clay. 'I will put hot coal in here to keep you warm,' says she. 'And take my cloak, my duck, and the little bread we have left.'

'And mutton, Sister,' wheedles Hugh, hastening to the pot above the fire.

My mother sets a cap upon my head and binds her scarf around it, tight under my face and round my neck. And then she binds my shoes with cloth. 'To keep the wet snow from your little feet,' she says, her voice so soft, as I used to hear it as a little one, but she does not beg me back to her hearthside. She lets me go. Yet she will learn thus to love me again. I am sure of it.

And so I step out into the stealthy snow. And still she does not call me back.

'Shelley? Shelley!'

Someone was coming up the hill towards her. She could not see clearly, so thick was the fall. She looked at the fragment of Blue John in her hand. The crocus colours had darkened, crimson-black, funereal. So was the sky dark, little light there now. It had released the pending snow in great circling flakes, not pretty, white, cotton wool snow, but snow that threatened and smothered.

Seven

'Come on home, duck!'

It was Matthew. He crouched down and draped Shelley's own coat on her shoulders. 'What are you thinking of, sitting up here in the snow? You're too nesh for this.'

Shelley couldn't tell him. Her head was full of Addie and her mother and her dissembling brother, of Addie's hunger for love. Addie's plan was crazy! She thought of William Harvey and his poor idiot daughter.

Matthew reached out to pull her up. His hands were always warm, she thought. 'What have you got there?' he asked.

She put the glass wing in his hand.

'Mmm. A bit of Blue John,' he said. 'That's mined Castleton way. It's been cut too. It looks as if it's been joined to another bit, then lost. How odd, I should keep that. Tourist tat shop would give you a few quid for it.'

She shook her head.

'Or you could have it made into a brooch. There's a nice silversmith at Wirksworth would do it.' He took it from her and peered at it. 'It's been on a string,' he said. 'There's a hole.' He gave it back, gently turning her hand safe over it. He asked, 'You all right, Shelley?'

'Yes,' she murmured. 'But I was just thinking, when the mist or the snow come down here, you could be in any time. It puts the world on hold. It's like that funny old film, where the Scottish village disappears into the mist. Your village, trapped high in that cleft. Kings and gods spread mist, didn't they, to hide their secret places? I can imagine your old locals believing in witches casting mist over their village. All that superstition and suspicion.'

'All right, Ms Sophistication. So, we're all a bit fossilised,' he said. 'Rock-bound, that's us. Rock doesn't give a lot. There's people quarrying and digging up half of our lands for motorways, and carting it off by the lorry load. They've dug out the minerals, like your Blue John, and the lead.'

'But there's no lead now?'

'No. Lead mining went like coal did for the poor coal miners. They started to import the stuff cheaper.'

'Must have been a rotten life,' said Shelley.

'Yeah. Of course, being an intellectual and into literature, you'll know the Daniel Defoe bit about the lead miner? The woman living with her five children in the cave?'

'No,' said Shelley, thinking, Show-off.

'"Lean as a skeleton and pale as a dead corpse . . . flesh of the same colour as the lead itself"?'

'No, I've never heard that,' she said firmly. 'Here, put your coat back on.'

'Thanks. C'mon, let's get back. Of course, it was God's plan, poverty.'

She smiled. 'All that hardness,' she said.

'Yeah,' Matthew said. 'It's as if the rock wants to keep everything for itself. There's archaeologists have found rock graves. They found what they call Beaker Folk sitting in the hillsides. Always makes me think of vending machines with little cartoon figures. They're end of the Bronze Age. They've even found buried children. Tell you what,' he added, as he took her hand to help her over the stile, 'all this rock makes farming hard.'

What was she doing with a farmer's boy? Yesterday she'd seen that other man, someone with style and mystery, and money no doubt. Matthew turned to Shelley again and smiled, those dark eyes gleaming, his clear skin weathered brown even now, stippled blue-black where he shaved. He made her think of beechnuts and forest floors. She didn't want to. She wanted to see someone tall with eyes blue as a Greek sea and hair of moonshine. The yachtsman. Matthew was too pushy. He seemed to assume he was looking after her when she had never even asked him to.

She said, 'How can you stand the farm smell?'

He laughed. 'You get used to it. It's the grass, that's all. My mum always says they should market a washing-powder specially to get cow muck out of clothes. Imagine the adverts! When I was twelve or thirteen, I used to get all embarrassed if I had mardy friends back. They'd comment on the smell, glance around themselves, go, "Pooh! What's that pong?" Now I don't bother about it. I just get in the shower with my Mr Muscle body rub.' He grinned at her, and she looked away quickly from the image of the brown skin on his shoulders, wet from the steam.

'Shall we see a film tonight?' he said, by the cottage.

'I don't fancy driving out in this snow,' she said.

'This snow? This is nothing! A dusting of icing sugar, that's all. No problem for the Land-Rover. No problem for the driver, either. Let me show you my off-road skills, my dear.'

Boasting again, thought Shelley. Where does all his confidence come from? What does he think he's got?

'No, I just wouldn't feel safe,' she said, satisfied when she saw the light in his eyes dimmed.

'All right,' he said. He seemed to recover very quickly. 'We'll go somewhere on foot instead. I want you to meet somebody. Come on.'

They turned at the top of the street, above the slated cat-slide roofs and the stone stairs creeping up the cottage sides, and there was the squat church, sitting in the circle of flakes as if it were trapped in the clear plastic of a child's snowstorm.

'It'll be locked,' Shelley said.

'It won't. Not now. My uncle's a churchwarden and it's bell practice, ready for New Year.'

The churchyard was steep and thick with carious stones, leaning like trees into the wind, some toppled and fallen. The flakes clung and melted on their darkness, smudging the letters. There were gravestones laid down in front of the porch, too. You had to walk over the writing to get in to the church.

Matthew turned the handle in the heavy door. Cold struck up from the slabs, but near the pews, hot pipes belted out heat.

'Vicar's decided heating needed turning up,' said Matthew. 'After all, he's been doing overtime this past week or two. Good little church, isn't it? Eight hundred years old.'

Shelley stood in the aisle, looking round to see bright embroidered cushions and white and bronze flowers and even a small garden of stones and plants and ponds.

'It's got a nice feel,' she whispered, she couldn't help herself whispering. 'It feels of people. I don't like churches much usually. They threaten me.'

'Shouldn't do,' said Matthew. 'Lots of good things have happened around here. Births, marriages. Holidays and festivals, prayers and thanks for deliverance from wars and plagues. If you didn't come here you were quite cut off, cut off from the heart. Here and the alehouse, of course. They handled all the money in the alehouse.'

He took a step backwards and gazed up at the windows. 'The daylight's too poor to see the colours in the glass. Shame. See the lead miner?'

In one window walked a man with a pick, like a child's drawing, stick legs and large feet, a white face under a brown brimless hat. Shelley thought of Addie's father coughing and without breath.

And then the bells began, an inevitable, tumultuous peal. The sound throbbed at her head, first one side, and then to the other side, and back, in time, to the first side as if her head itself was a bell. She turned desperately to Matthew who had his hands clapped over his ears.

'I should have warned you,' he shouted. 'Bell practice. They get a bit carried away.'

All around the air hummed and vibrated. How many resonances over how many years were caught and held in the dense walls, Shelley thought wildly, just as the stone in the stairwell trapped water, and words, and held them there.

Matthew staggered to the back of the church in a hump-backed shape, hands clawing at the air and croaking, 'The bells! The bells! This way, my dear.'

He beckoned her behind a curtain and up a little stone staircase. There was a pause in the peals of bells. Folk stood by ropes, preoccupied, while Matthew and Shelley scrambled up a metal ladder, steep, up through a trap door.

'Here he is,' said Matthew.

At first she noticed nothing. Opposite them was a whitewashed wall. Then she saw, in the wall, a stone. On the stone was a little man. He was plain, crude, a relief carving worn away by time. There were no features, no feet even, but his right arm was bent at the elbow as if his hand rested on his chest.

'Who is he?' she asked.

'No one really knows,' said Matthew. 'He's very old, older than

Christianity. Of course, Christianity reached here later than other places.'

'Of course,' said Shelley.

'He was found a few miles away, and his stone was brought here and built into this bell tower. That was in the twelfth century, and if they thought he was special enough to move *then*, he's – er, he's something.'

'He's extraordinary,' breathed Shelley. The world was rolling back away from her, she could not consider all that time, all that darkness, and this little pagan figure somehow withstanding all that change and joy and horror.

'He's such a merry little man,' she said.

'Yes. He's my very favourite guy,' said Matthew. 'I've always liked him, right from being a kid. His face is worn away, but I know he's smiling. And his hand is on his heart.'

'Then his heart is very low down,' said Shelley.

'Perhaps they weren't too hot on anatomy in his time,' retorted Matthew. 'I say his hand is on his heart. My dad says his hand's on his belly 'cos he's just had a good meal. I won't tell you where my little brother thinks the hand is.'

She sniggered. 'Adam would say the same,' she said.

'Come on, Shelley, I'll buy you a drink. And I must come and meet this skylark sometime. Is it kept in your room?'

'Yes. I leave the bedside lamp on to keep her warm.'

'It's a her, is it? Suppose it would have to be,' he said.

Matthew held Shelley's arm as she teetered down the slippery path through the churchyard and into the lane towards the pub. The cold air was rich with woodsmoke. It was good to be here.

'Whoops! You were nearly down then!' cried Matthew, clamping his arm round her waist. At least he could keep her from falling.

She felt an elastic band of excitement tighten across her stomach. Perhaps the yachtsman would be in the pub, his hair as fair as an angel's in the dark of the bar.

'Mind out!' cried Matthew.

A little old tractor lurched to a stop in the middle of the narrow street. Its engine consisted mostly of string and a lemonade bottle. No number plate. A bale of straw and an old collie with an eye white as an egg sat on the back.

'Sam Ferane,' announced Matthew as the crouched figure fell out of the cab and flapped into the pub. 'Drinks here every day. Has done since he was twelve, apparently.'

'How old is he?' asked Shelley, stepping towards the collie but changing her mind as it curled its lip from a yellow tooth.

'Oh, eighty-seven, eighty-eight, you know. He's a real boy racer, mind. Steer clear of his tractor when he's sloshed or he'll run you down.'

'Is it him who slops down the hill in his dressing-gown and slippers?'

'Dressing-gown? Oh, no. You mean his baby brother, Walter. Walt the stonemason. Does a bit of freelance grave-digging too, difficult round here with all the rocks. Only room for a few in the churchyard, then you have to go elsewhere!'

'Don't be horrible, Matthew,' she said.

'Just a fact of life, my dear. Old Walter and Sam always sound like they're fighting, though we don't think they are, it's just their way of going on. Haven't you ever heard them shouting? Their voices ring right across the village.'

'No,' said Shelley. 'I'm glad to say those are voices I *haven't* heard.'

Matthew stopped and looked at her and she knew she would not get away before she'd explained herself. He wanted to know. 'What voices?' he asked.

'Oh, just stories.'

'Stories? D'you read a lot?'

'Yes, but that's nothing to do with it!' she said. 'I'm sort of aware of some people from the past.'

'You mean, reincarnation?'

'No-o! They're not me. They're nothing to *do* with me. They pick on me to tell their stories to.'

'Sounds fun. Why not?'

'Why not? WHY NOT? What do *you* think? I've never told Mum, but I told my real father about voices I heard when I was little and – '

'And what? What did he say?'

She rolled her eyes. 'Can't you guess? He said no one was there and I shouldn't tell people about it. He meant they'd think I was schizophrenic, didn't he, mad, bonkers, insane, doolally, and I wonder if he's right.'

'Rubbish,' he said. 'Mum hears folk, I told you, and she takes it for what it is.'

You're wrong, thought Shelley, she feels odd about it, I know she does.

'Mum doesn't go on about spooks flapping in white sheets. It's just another sense she has. You can scoff with your brother, Shelley, but there's no certainty about time. I don't see why energy shouldn't hang around, and some people have the gift to hear it.'

'Gift?' She felt tears pricking her eyelids. 'It's a curse, not a gift. And it's worse since I've been in your cottage, and up that hill. Two girls now, they seek me out, me! And I tell you something, Matthew Harvey, *your* name crops up in the last story I was told!'

He shrugged and Shelley felt even crosser. 'Not surprising if a few old Harveys crop up in your story, Shelley. The Harveys have lived here for centuries. There've been lots of 'em. And there'll be more. More of them in stories for the future.'

'You can't take anything seriously, can you?' she snapped. 'These voices, these girls or young women, I don't know how old they are exactly, but one must have been a teenager when the other one was born, they . . . they just want to be heard, to offload their stories, make themselves feel better. I mean I feel sorry for them but – '

'Perhaps they're not just telling their stories to help themselves,' Matthew whispered. 'Perhaps you should listen a bit closer sometimes, Shelley.'

He tipped up her wet face and brushed her cheek with a warm hand, that damaged hand. 'Come on, let's get out of the cold. Now,' he said, going to hold open the pub door for her, 'what'll you have?'

'Bacardi and Coke,' she said quickly, thinking reluctantly, he could be right. There are strands in their stories of fathers and mothers and brothers, much that's similar to my life.

A fire leaped in the grate, flickering dark orange against the oak settles and tables. Behind the bar stood the landlord, a huge man with his head set well down into his shoulders. His head moved from side to side, like an adder, as he watched Shelley, a stranger. Then he saw Matthew and his face relaxed into recognition. Matthew took her to sit by the great stone fireplace. The only other person she could see was old Sam Ferane, shrunk in his high-backed settle, face sunk into his coat collar under his brimless leather hat.

And a low voice, a woman's voice. Pleading. 'I cannot pay. For pity's sake, I cannot pay.'

'I'll pay for you,' cried Shelley.

'I cannot pay for the headstones. How can I bury my little ones without them?'

But when Shelley turned, there was no woman there. No, only old Sam Ferane shrunk in his high-backed settle, face hidden. No one else.

'Who are you talking to?' asked Matthew.

'No one,' she said.

'Do you want something to eat, too?' asked Matthew. He took her long dark plait from her collar and smoothed it down her back. 'Your hair's got little snow crystals on it,' he said. 'Come on, Shelley, you'll fade away. Eat.'

'No, thanks.'

'Not even if I ask you sweetly?' he whispered, and he danced before her with his hand on his heart like the little stone man. She laughed, she could not help herself.

'See the Derbyshire specialities on the blackboard?' he said. 'Garlic mushrooms, vegetable curry, Greek salad, chicken on ratatouille.'

She giggled. 'I'll have vegetable curry, please.'

'Right. Mine's Greek salad and chips. Maybe the Harveys should breed more sheep again and go into feta farming,' he said, moving to the bar.

Eight

Shelley couldn't forget the girl in the mine. That night, as she listened to the wind gusting down the valley, Shelley pictured the little girl, Addie, rocked warm on her mother's knee, listening to stories of the great dragon who breathed fire in the storm. But what a way to try to win your mother's love, by taking the blame for your wretched brother! Were they really that cruel to her? Did they really shut her out, was that true? Or was her jealousy changing her story, casting her as the loveless heroine?

Shelley sat up in the half-light and put her hand to her ribs. She could feel Addie's loneliness as an ache. It was no good. She had to know what happened.

She pulled back the curtains. Grey light, intangible as the light before a film. The snow was falling thick and fast as duck down. Shelley ate a piece of toast and set out again for the mine head. She stood in the eerie white spaces as the snow spun round her, waiting for the girl to take up her story once again. She heard murmuring, like running water, the distant twittering of birds and then that soft voice:

My mother will learn thus to love me again, I'm sure of it . . . Three steps outside the door and our house is lost to me for ever. Perhaps these flaws chase me only and do not fall elsewhere. They whirl me in a cage of white. The moon gives light, I trust it will not be enough to show me to the folk in Upper Town.

I struggle up the hillside, towards the mine. Addie's Fortune! And so it will be.

The spinning snow puts me in mind of faces in a pressing crowd, the day my father took me to the fair. We ate hot gingerbread, we watched the people play cards and race their pigs, saw booths set with the wares of silversmiths and milliners. The air smelled foreign to us, of rich coffee and the brandy shops. We sought the books. (It was my father taught me how to read, for only Hugh might go to school.)

We saw sellers of medicines, magic for the banishing of warts, but not a tincture for my poor face. The May morning dew had never healed it. Yet Father says my cowpox will keep me from catching the deathly smallpox now, and for that I must be thankful, says he. And so I try to be.

We watched the toothdrawers working on their

reluctant clients. They sold their teeth of ivory, bone and hippopotamus tusk, but my father laughed and said he would have none of them. Father bought me an orange! I had never dreamed such sweetness as I tasted that day.

The fair fades. I am back inside my cage of snow.

The mine head gapes, like the mouth leading down to Hell, yet above it the hill wears its coxcomb of ash and rowan to keep away evil. I trust in their power now! And I wonder if the candle burns there still, the candle left at Christmas to appease the spirit of the mine? This spirit leads the true miner to his fortune, tapping its way to the rich veins of lead, the miner and his daughter, for it was I, not Hugh, who helped Father. I knocked and washed the ore at the mine head. The lead sells well for the rich to roof their great houses and, in great hopes, my father named his new mine for me. Addie's Fortune!

Now the mouth of the mine is rimmed silver with gathering snow. When the snow melts, the mine will flood . . . but I will not be there then, my mother will have come to call me back, I know it!

I crawl into the coe. Some of my father's working clothes wait here for his return. I know his cap of rabbit-skin is here, and his linsey drawers. I will not look. Here is a candle-holder of bottle glass, with the larger part of a candle there. It will keep the dark at bay! Yet I dare not light it now lest they see.

Darkness draws me in. Whether to harbour me, or from malevolence, I do not know.

And then I hear a noise.

Listen.

Someone is already come in my pursuit! They –

The voice stopped, suddenly. Shelley waited, straining to hear it against the stealthy snow and the occasional call from the village. Nothing.

Shelley crunched slowly down the hill, and stood dripping in the porch as Matthew arrived. She brought the bird down to him, more confident now, no longer fearful that the bird's bones would snap like dried spaghetti. The skylark seemed stronger. It turned its head and its eyes gleamed dark as elderberries.

'Maybe a sparrowhawk had it awhile, then let it fall,' mused Matthew, touching the wing lightly. 'I've never seen one grounded like this before. I'm amazed it hasn't died.'

Shelley felt happily smug. She said, 'Perhaps she was just weak for some reason. She doesn't seem wounded. Anyway, she's much better today. Adam looked out his plastic tank for her to live in, look.'

'Good for Adam! Well, I can't see any blood on the bird. Looks fine. You need to let it go.'

'What, in this snow?' she cried.

'How do you think they usually manage, Shelley? They live through peak winters, most of 'em anyway. It's a wild thing. Let it go in the morning or it won't stand it, being shut in. I'm amazed it

69

has anyway. You must have the right touch.' His eyes, so dark she could not see their centres, sought her own and her face grew warm.

'Anyway,' he said softly, coaxing, 'it'll be a bit warmer tomorrow, you'll see.'

'Old country lore, is it, Matthew?'

'Old weather report lore on radio. I'll bring the bird over a bit of seed later, some sprouting shoots'll do her good. Maybe I'll find a few little insects.'

Shelley put the bird back upstairs and went to see Matthew out. His boots squeaked on the new snow, and the sheepdog raced down the hill from Linnet Farm to greet him. He bent to fuss it, then it ran at his side, looking up at his face. Why could those dogs never just walk, thought Shelley.

She turned to find Adam the Unspeakable, Adam the Inevitable, standing in the porch, arms folded, watching.

'Too nice, poor sod,' he said. 'Too available, that's his disadvantage. Too normal and straight, not some snotty cardboard cut out who drives a flashy car.'

'Shut up, Adam, you interfering moron! Go and flush yourself out of my life,' she shouted and pushed past him into the cottage.

'Hello darling,' sang her mother. 'Sibling sweetness again? I'm glad Matthew found you, Shell. Such a pleasant lad. Still, saying that won't help his cause, will it? Dave and I thought we might wander up the other end of the village when the snow stops. Have a look at the house.'

Shelley rolled her eyes heavenwards. 'They won't be working on it today, Mother. Not till after New Year.'

'I know that, darling, but I thought we might measure up a bit, start planning for carpets and curtains. Then I can hit the sales next week.' She rubbed her hands together in glee. 'I can't wait to get in there and put my mark on it.' She stopped and looked at her daughter. 'Aren't you excited, lovey! New bedroom? Choosing all the stuff from scratch?'

Shelley turned and threw a log onto the fire.

'Not even a bit excited, love?' said her mother. She was almost pleading.

'No,' said Shelley smugly.

She *was* looking forward to the new house. It was a so-called architect-designed executive number. Stone-built, of course, not too out of character with the rest of the village. It had the works, according to the blurb, fitted breakfast kitchen with antique oak, forest green Aga, palatial utility room, downstairs cloakroom, dining room and lounge complete with countless niches for television, video and phone. There was a study, master bedroom with en suite bathroom and fitted furniture, three further bedrooms, family bathroom with whirlpool bath and three-piece suite (in oyster), a decent-sized secluded garden, and garaging for three cars, even if you only had one. Shelley had heard her mother going on about it so often that she could parrot the details.

But Shelley recognised in herself an anticipation about the house, an exhilarated nervousness. Shelley did not want an interrogation from her mother. She wanted to go back and sit alone with her bird, so she left the fire and opened the door to the stairs.

'Ugh!' she shouted. 'Never mind the new house, Mother. When are we going to get rid of this stink?'

She had forgotten about Joanie. She bawled the second Shelley set foot on the stair. Shelley did not have to strain to catch this cawing as she had to hear Addie's soft sentences.

'Ere, listen, will yer? Will yer?

Yer will.

Swank pot, they call me. Gabbletraps. 'Listen, gabbletraps. Don't go near that mine.' That is Addie's Fortune no more! It's Harvey's mine, now Fayther's married Johnson's widder. She's brought 'er chaff bed out today and 'er little house beyond Crow Wood stands empty. Some vagabond'll 'ave it.

Me fayther's new wife is a poor mezzled thing. Me brothers keep laughing, they say Fayther always wanted 'er, and now he's got the mine, too. That dead Buxton man thought himself above us, and lost it all. She 'as a son, Hugh, a nazzy britches, and I mun call him Uncle Hugh. She 'ad a bit of pewter and a few shillings, and the mine. 'Don't go there,' she begs me, clinging on my hand. 'Don't go up there, I beg yer, Addie.' Gormless barmpot. I'm Joan.

Well, one day I did go. I knew no one was working

the mine. Me brothers were at their band, wi' fiddle and hautboy, and Fayther and her were up at top end of village thinkin' on their new farmhouse. It were to be all shells and flowers on the ceiling, and glass in the winders, never mind tax! Fayther says the mine will pay for it.

So off I go, up the hill, to have a look at this mine and see what's so precious. I climb down a little, just a small way, so dark, dark. I don't know what I thought I'd find. I never thought I'd find a skeleton! There it was in the very fost coffin level, bleached and pale like a ghost, but with bones. Bones.

I was back up as fast as I could, and look who's there! Look who's stuck his big head before me in the shaft. Uncle Hugh. He was slottened. He was allus slottened, that one. His voice had gone off, he's not so high above us as he thinks!

He says, 'I saw you comin' oop 'ere. Yer'll cop it round t'ear-'ole if yer fayther and me mam find out.'

Clack-fart. I'm afeared of me fayther. He has a rage on him like a roof-fall.

He says, Uncle Hugh, that is, he says, 'Yer face is red, Joanie. What's oop?'

'There's bones,' I gasps.

His face darkens, blood-dark. 'No,' he growls.

'Yes,' I says. 'I think it's a dog.'

'Thank God,' he says. He looks at me and I don't like it. His eyes is all gleamy and I want to go 'ome, but, 'Come here, Joanie,' he wheedles. 'Yer lookin' right pretty.'

Slorm-pot. He pulls me up, and into the coe. Then he lifts me skirt, me homespun, and giggles, goes, 'Duck-footed Joanie, yer little loosher.'

'No, Uncle Hugh, leave me,' I says and struggle but he pushes me down. It's cowd. He stinks of ale, an' his eyes is all wavy red and blue, like little bits of blue stone.

'You like it, Joanie, you little loosher,' he slobbers, an' I don't know what he's doin' but I don't like it, I don't, an' I know he shouldn't a done it, it were like bein' cut in half by a sword and I screams and he goes, 'I'll thrape thee Joan! Lie still.'

After, when I'm so hurtin' , and cryin', and stinkin', he says, 'And don't yer say a word, gabbletraps. I'll say yer wanted it. I'll say yer begged me for it. They'll never believe yer, 'cos yer a not-mucher.'

And he leaves me there, all bruises and tears and slithery between me legs.

I hope he dies blathered in blood, hope the Devil eats him, wobblin' great legs and Black Jack eyes and all. Kith and kin?

No one ever listens to Joanie. No one hears. I'm here at back of stairs. We both are, waitin'.

*

Shelley stood frozen on the stairs, hands clenched into fists. Joanie's voice had stopped abruptly. Feeling sick from Joanie's humiliation, Shelley climbed slowly to her room. She skimmed the bird's head with one finger and the skylark tried to stretch her wings.

The snow had fallen and settled, and fallen again. The hillside outside her window hung, floating like a huge pantomime ghost in a sheet. The silence was blissful to Shelley, masking Joan's pain. The eiderdown of snow seemed to have smothered everything. Not her mother's voice, though. No snowfall could muffle that.

'Shelley?' her mum called. 'Shelley! Shell-EEEE! Shelley, come down.'

'Why?'

'Because.'

'Oh, Mother, what is it?'

'There's a letter for you. Sent on from the old house.'

'A letter for me?'

'Yes. It arrived this morning, sorry, I forgot to give it to you.'

Shelley put the skylark back in her container, threw open her bedroom door and caught the top of her head on the roof as she hurtled down the little stairs and pushed past her mother into the sitting room.

'Where is it?' she cried, spinning round.

'On the table.'

Shelley snatched the envelope and ripped at the top, and as she ran out she shouted, 'Next time you go shopping, Mother dear, get one of those floral bomb things to kill the stink on that stair!'

Nine

Shelley raced upstairs to her room and slammed the door shut. Her father's letter was postmarked 19th December, all that time ago. She had written to him in November. Of course, she thought, excusing him, she had been in Scotland, they'd had a break away.

Perhaps this letter had invited her to come at Christmas, at least for some of the time. His mind would have been on her for a little while. Mo could deal with the children, Noah and Daisy, just for once, couldn't she? All this new man bit was fine, but what about his other daughter, his first daughter, Shelley, what about new manning it for her? When Shelley was small he worked all the time, late into the evenings and at weekends. She just couldn't remember him being there. He was busy establishing the business, Mum said. That was part of the trouble between them. Mum was left holding the baby, and when the first baby was reasonably independent, she had another one to hold. Adam. Shelley had to become really independent then!

Now he shared everything about his new family: hunts for the most absorbent, least buttock-chafing nappies, vigils at the playground to make sure they didn't decapitate themselves under the roundabout, treks to and from nursery, anthems of 'Ooh!' and 'Aah!' at each wobbly construction of cardboard rolls and cereal boxes they brought home, and each painting so sodden with paint it had to be dried curling on top of the storage heater. On her last visit he'd been making a list for Mo, planning their daughter's birthday party, writing down games and things to eat, bouncy castle and party bags, and a prize for pass the parcel. He'd pulled on a pirate hat over his silvering hair while he wrote; the children loved that, and so did Shelley. Had he done that on *her* birthday?

He was still better-looking than other dads, even the younger dads, she thought. Tall, always well-dressed, casual but with an eye for texture and colour, just like damnable Adam. The eyes, blue as cornflowers speckled with gold, and the dark, thick hair were just like Adam, yet they weren't close. Adam didn't seem to miss his father at all. He'd only been to visit once, years ago, and had not minded that Shelley subsequently went alone.

'*Dear Shelley . . .*' her eyes sped on, although she wanted to slow them down, to linger over each word. '*Thank you for your letter. Christmas will be fun for you this year, I'm sure. Being a stupid old fool of a male, I don't know what to buy a beautiful girl of 17, so here is a cheque, which I hope will be acceptable. I'm sure you'll have a wonderful festive season. Hope the move goes well. That is a super part of the countryside, isn't it? A bit remote for me, but I'm sure you'll like it.*

We're going to be very busy over Christmas. Mo's parents are coming, and of course we'll have our hands full with the small terrors! Think what a narrow escape you've had! Shell, I know you're old enough to understand now. Mo just wants us to have a family Christmas. Just her parents, and me, and the children.'

But *I'm* one of your children, Dad! *I'm* part of your family Christmas. And where's the next invitation, where's the invite for half-term or Easter? How many hints do I need to drop? In my letter I wrote, *'Please let me come to stay. I could help with Noah and Daisy. It would be fun.'*

Shelley blinked hard. His words were becoming blurred and splodgy. She read,

'Congratulations on your acceptance for university. Such a clever girl! Only two low grades will be no problem for you, I remember you got a couple of A grades in your GCSEs.'

I have to get three exams, not two. And I got seven A grades in my GCSEs, Dad.

'Head down and work, my dear. Your mother never finished her degree. Make sure you do! No mucking about, now, and none of your flights of fancy once you get to Cambridge!'

It's Oxford.

He signed off, *Declan*.

A tear fuzzed the 'e' in Declan. Shelley dropped the cheque on the bed. There was a soft knocking on the door. Shelley ignored it, but the latch was lifted and the door opened quietly and there stood her mum.

'I knew you'd come up here on your own, dear' she said. 'You always did like to hide away, to scuttle off and bury yourself. Even as a little girl. You used to make dens and hideaways anywhere, out of sheets and clothes airers and under trees and even behind the stairs.' Her mother smiled at the memories, then the smile faded. She said, 'Closing yourself off from me. Full of secrets. We need to talk, you know, we never do. We skirt round each other. We need to take deep breaths and try again.' Her nose gave its little rabbit twitch, then hesitantly, she held out her arms. Shelley pushed past her and saw her mother's arms fall slowly. They'd both known Shelley would not fill them. She saw her mother's face crumple with disappointment, and felt a small pang for her, but that wasn't the worst thing. Somehow Shelley couldn't help herself, her mother had to be disappointed, that had to happen. It was her father's rejection that was the worst thing of all.

Shelley ran downstairs and wrenched open the door to the porch, and the street door.

'Oi, Shelley!' cried Dave from the sofa. 'Please don't leave the door open, love. There's a howling gale.'

'You're letting in the snow, you daft cow!' shrieked Adam.

Shelley didn't hear them. She held the letter up in front of her face, then ripped off every little corner, letting each one be lifted out of her hand to flutter away with the snowflakes. It was like throwing very expensive confetti. Her father loved beautiful things, and this paper would be from his business, probably handmade, she thought with satisfaction. The paper was whirled fast away until she let the very last piece go, into the snowstorm, down the street, across the valley, who knew where, words in wisps and threads.

Shelley came back inside, shut both doors behind her and stood in front of the fire. She warmed the back of her legs while the rest of her body shook with cold.

'How much d'ya get then?' asked Adam, sensitive as ever to her feelings. 'He sent me twenty quid. Same as we got last year, isn't it?'

She ignored him.

'C'mon, Shelley,' came Dave's soft, middle-of-the-range voice. She scowled at him as he bulged on the sofa, Humpty Dumpty in man-made fibres. 'Try not to let the anger take you over like that.'

'They won't ask me to stay,' she said, head down to hide the tears. 'Something is stopping him. It's Mo. Mo and the children. Or he thinks I'm weird. You've been saying things, haven't you, Mum, saying things about me to him?'

'I've hardly talked to the man for years!' cried her mother.

'Shelley, stop giving yourself such a bad press. You're not weird,' soothed Dave. He adjusted his glasses so that Shelley could see his eyes over the top of them. His eyes were quite large and blue. 'You're one very bright lady. You're a little bit inward-looking, but what's wrong with that? There are enough braggarts and empty vessels in the world already. The man is preoccupied, that's all. You can't hang on to him. You must settle with us now, Shelley.'

'He couldn't remember my grades, or anything. He doesn't LISTEN!'

There was a long silence. Then, 'Now *that* could have been a family trait.' That was Dave speaking. She heard her mother's soft snort of laughter, and couldn't take it.

Shelley shot Dave a look full of poisoned darts. He shrugged his rounded shoulders and the darts didn't stick. He said, 'Perhaps you expend sadness where it's not needed, Shelley, and miss out elsewhere. Perhaps you hurt too much. There is much more in your life, you know, much more going on now and in the near future, never mind what's already happened. We can be sorry, but we can't really change it.'

She blinked against the heat of the tears, from far away heard her mother's voice, brightening, hoping she'd hit a good note. 'There's a do on at the sailing clubhouse tomorrow night. We can all go, it'll do us good. There'll be food and we can have a bit of a bop.'

'Yeah, Billy Harvey and his family are going!' cried Adam. 'And you'll be able to boogie with oiks from the sailing club, Sister Shell!'

Shelley felt she should shout at him, but she had not the strength to get angry. New Year's Eve, she thought dully, supposed to be a new beginning . . . She was limp, empty, drained, undermined. She dragged herself up the stairs to be with her bird. She could still smell Joan. And then she heard that voice, a little weaker, and full of pain:

Are yer listenin'?

They never saw, they never noticed, they were too bound up with theirselves. All that time, all those months. I had nobody to tell. Nobody to listen.

I felt so bad that mornin'. I left the house and went up the mine again, I knew Uncle Hugh would not follow me for he was abed, too much ale the neet before. It were New Year's Eve, they were not workin' the mine that day, they were up at the farmhouse, but I were there, crouched there, they might just as well 'ave shoved their picks up me for the pain I knew. I bit me lips until they dripped, mustn't scream, they might come, and then in a rush something slithered out of me, and a great dollop of blood. I knew what it was, but it 'adn't 'ad long enough, yersee, it wasn't right.

I was thirteen. It's too young to have a babby, I know that now. Fost I thought it was the Divil's babby, to put it in a Divil box and pass it on, for he was like the Divil, was Uncle Hugh. But it were so little. Littler than a lamb, little as a songbird over the pasture. And it were dead. It were a little girl.

I kept pokin' the babby, I put 'er to my breast, although there were nowt there for 'er to suck, I knew I hadn't growed 'er long enough.

I cut that rope with me brooch and tied it neat, I knew you did that. I wrapped the babby in me cloak and ran to Wormhill. There's the old stone there, with the big hole that heals. I passed 'er to and fro in and out of that stone, back and forrards. But she would not live.

I put 'er in the mine.

I climbed down a little way, only a little, I hurt so much yersee. And I put 'er on a ledge. I could not take 'er home, not on New Year's Day, yer must not take anything in and out of the house that day, even yer chamber pot nor yer ashes from the fire. It brings bad luck. So I left 'er in the mine that day, and I went home and I were cryin'.

'What's oop?' asked me fayther but I didn't tell, just took to me bed till the morrow. Then I was up to the mine afore any on 'em, and I fetched 'er home, where she should be. And I put 'er under the stairs.

I sit there with 'er so she shan't be alone. I feel bad, so bad. And the blood won't stop. Sometimes it's red as Robin Red-breast, sometimes dark as Divil's blood.

Don't trust 'em, any on 'em. I feel so bad, so bad, so . . . And I put 'er under the stairs . . .

Joan said no more.

Shelley climbed the stairs slowly, feeling sick with shock, thinking, thirteen, a dead baby. Blood.

She sat on her bed for a while, and then pulled herself up to search for her little photograph album in the drawer. She felt uneasy. There was the photo of Dad, handsome and smiling. Other photos too, mostly of birthday parties when she was little. Shelley had been photographed cutting cakes or waving balloons, the Unspeakable usually hovering as high as her waist, grinning to charm anyone who glanced his way.

But not her dad. He was never there.

Ten

Before dawn Shelley woke with a jolt. The skylark sat peering round through its clear plastic walls. It fluffed up its feathers and gave a little tremble. Then it startled Shelley by making a little run across the tank. It didn't hop as she might have thought. Matthew had called back last night with a mix of grain, sprouted seeds and the odd insect, and most of this had disappeared; on the floor of the container there was a large swirly dropping to explain this disappearance.

'Today's freedom day, little one!' whispered Shelley. She pulled warm clothes over her pyjamas and crept downstairs, carrying the bird in its container. 'I'll just make a hot drink,' she told it, and put tea in a thermos to drink up on the pasture.

Fresh snow squeaked under her wellingtons as she climbed in the half-light to the very top of the skull hill, to the Mohican crest by the mine, and there set down the container. She lifted the bird out, put her lips to the tiny head in a kiss and then opened her hands.

A split second's pause. Then the skylark fluttered like an insect and flew in a quite vertical line, until she dissolved into the sky.

'Into another world,' cried Shelley in delight. She'd done it. The bird was well and she was free! Shelley sat down by the mine and unscrewed the lid of her thermos flask.

I need a dog, she thought, suddenly lonely now her bird had flown. She remembered Joan trying to revive her dead bundle, passing it in and out of the Celts' other stone worlds, and Addie, hiding in the mine waiting for her mother. She could feel their loneliness shrouding the hill.

If I listen hard, I'll hear Addie, thought Shelley. I'll hear her mother and brother, Hugh, come to take her home.

And soon Addie's voice began, so different from Joan's. No wonder the Harveys thought Addie's family were snobs.

They are come in my pursuit. The noise is not made by human means. A black form throws itself at me! It is my little dog, Jack! He will not stay with my mother and Hugh but seeks his true mistress.

I scoop him up, loyal little creature, and he licks my face with his hot tongue.

My father would never let him here, for a black dog brings ill fortune to the mine. Now I hold his joyful body to my own, delighting in his love, for he loves only me.

'Eat this, dear Jack,' I whisper, my lips on his soft ear. I unwrap the cloth and feed him the mutton given to me by

Hugh, for I have no stomach for it. I eat a little bread. We wait.

The dawn, however dark, brings hope in midwinter. The sky is leaden, pending snow, but there is the sun to make his brief visit.

Far across the wastes are the shattered rocks, and the black tracery of Crow Wood near my mother's house. When she comes to set me at my liberty from this mine I will gather snowdrops from that wood. I will purify the house, ready for Candlemas and the cleansing of the Virgin Mary, and mine own.

I hear the lowing of the cows in their byres. A cockerel crows. They will come to plead with me for my return, I know it.

In the valley the roofs sit like the white wings of waiting birds. There is no lamplight to be seen, for the windows are shuttered as if they have dropped eyelids, masking their secrets. I do not know of their inhabitants. My father kept us apart from this village. We do not go there.

At the end of Maggot Lane, a tall house stands apart. It has a walled garden, and a number of byres; it is a house of many hearths, the house of a wealthy man, who does not wear his own hair and who has lace at his cuffs. At one small window, candlelight rounds to a dull yellow globe. It flickers awhile, then fades away.

A dog howls in his yard, so cold a sound across these snowy wastes, so that my Jack shivers and hides his nose under my arm.

Then I hear hoofbeats. They recede. Silence. No, again they come, muffled in snow, but surely there. Along Maggot Lane comes a dark horse, forging through the snow, a rider sitting tall upon its back.

The horse and his rider disappear behind a long byre. I wait what seems an age and then out they come again. The horse picks its way as if it steps on glass. They stop. The rider sits still as stone. The horse snorts, blows out his cloud of ice crystals.

Who could be riding here? That is no poor miner's horse.

They are waiting where the road forks. One way leads to villages and the town, the other turns to the hill, then vanishes.

The rider turns his head, stares up the hillside. His heels twitch and the horse puts down his head, turns this way and plunges forward, surges up the hill, past the strip fields with their ridges rilled by snow, and halts. The rider slides down its flank to make his way on foot.

And then I know him! I know him by his great height in his black cloak. I see his head in the thick hood, set forward, move from side to side as a serpent might seek and search. And by this characteristic I know him at once.

It is the Barmaster, Barmaster Crawley, the most powerful man in our surrounds!

My father said that Crawley was a greedy man. He owns the alehouse, he is constable too, he has many lands and cows and hens, and mines. On this inclement dawn, he has come to claim my father's mine, he has come to nick the stows again with his knife, to make that mark to show that no one has worked this mine since Father died, for Hugh does not come near it. If the stows are nicked three times, the mine is lost to us, for there are many in the village who want it for themselves.

And Barmaster Crawley will find me! I have always feared him, he has a face that is cold as ice, he has that man's look without mercy or tenderness, as if he only sees what he can use.

I slip and slide into the mine mouth, down the shaft, as far as ever I dare. The depths of the earth are unnatural to me. I have never worked far down in the galleries and coffin levels for I cannot breathe there.

I close my eyes and wait. My little dog Jack lies still as death when he feels my terror.

I put my hand to touch the crystal Father gave me. I wear it always on leather at my throat and hold it in my hand when his absence pains me. It is a fine piece of Blue John, from the mines at Mam Tor, the mother mountain, the shivering mountain, the mountain that moves by herself. In the great houses they have expanses of this crystal with its strange bands of light, said my father. They scrub and store it, and polish it hard, and then dine off its table tops and stroke its cold urns with their soft, smooth hands, and burn their fires under mantels fashioned out of its fine bandings so that the light shines through. My father gave me two frail wings of this crystalline worked together; he said it is a butterfly from our brief summer. He said the colours run together like the scales on their small wings.

I fall into a half-sleep. I dream of springtime and soft wind up on the sheep runs and in the mist of bluebells in the wood, and then I dream my mother comes to call me home, as she did when I was a little girl. Then she would show me how to make a necklace from ox-eye flowers, and where there grew the blue stars of Jacob's ladders that the angels climb to heaven. In my dream my mother rocks me warm. There is no more blame for me. She smiles warm as lamplight and tells me Hugh has repented and been forgiven, that the Harveys bear no malice, that Hugh works Addie's Fortune well so that the poorhouse door does not stand wide for us. My mother tells me that she loves me.

I weep for joy and my little dog licks tears from my face, and then I come back out of my dream again into that cold dawn. Surely the Barmaster is gone, surely he is back at his hearthside now? My feet are numb. I try to see them as I place them on the holds up the climbing-shaft.

When at last I lift my face to the light I hear all too late the crunch of boots on snow. The daylight is taken. Between me and the sky snakes the hooded head of the Barmaster, sensing, moving from side to side.

Do not let him see me! Do not let him hear the thudding of my heart, for I can hear the rasping of his breath made louder in the mineshaft.

I cling there, eyes tight shut, fearing for my purity, fearing as the cold has stolen all feeling from my hands and feet, I will plunge down again into the mine depths.

My eyelids lighten. The shaft is bright again, the Barmaster is gone and I never know if he saw me or not. Till this day I am not sure.

I drag myself out to lie at the mine mouth, put up my hand to feel the butterfly but it is gone, it has been torn away from me, and I feel my father and my childhood flee with it.

In the sky there hangs a dark orange sun. It puts me in mind of the fair, and the sweetness, and the chattering people there.

I see the people coming up the hill. They are not merry, but vengeful, their shoulders set and their heads down against the cold. They are like beasts. They are coming for me.

I look round, wild, but can see no escape, unless I

throw myself to death down in the mine. If only I were a bird and could fly up and away into the heavens! I was foolish to think the Harveys would not hunt me down. At the foot of the hill, two figures watch. I see them. It is Hugh and my mother, come to watch my capture.

The people take me without struggle and carry my body down the hill, and it is only my dog cries for me from the mine.

Shelley shivered and wrapped her arms around her body. Addie was betrayed . . . she would be hanged, Shelley was sure that's what they did with thieves then! Surely they wouldn't let that happen . . . even if Hugh let Addie take the blame, her mother would repent.

But there was no more story. Shelley was left in a kind of limbo, as if the stories were not quite ended. Unless there was to be a rewind and another play for the next likely listener? Yet they chose me, she thought.

She felt as if everything existed in a state of waiting. It was as if the voices were still there, breathing softly. She tipped the last of her tea from the thermos onto the snow. The light brown crystals dissolved at once and vanished, leaving a little crater.

She stood up and brushed the snow from her coat. Better hurry back before more snow should fall and block her way.

Eleven

Mum and Dave were in the kitchen, faces close together, flushed. Shelley closed the door quietly behind her. Mum was murmuring to Dave. Shelley heard her say, 'But Dave, I must! She'll be going away soon. To university.'

Of course, thought Shelley. Not long and you'll be rid of me, and won't you be pleased, Mum! There'll be just you and Dave and Adam.

Too quickly her mother turned, saw her, called, 'Hi, Shelley! Let's live dangerously and put another tea bag in the pot. Fetch yourself a cup, love.'

No. Shelley shook her head and crossed to the stairwell. She went to her room and slept for a couple of hours, then had a hot bath and washed her hair. She wrapped her bathrobe tightly round her and began to plait her long wet hair in lots of small braids so that it would curl tightly and give her a soft mass in which to hide.

The voices in her head were quiet now. For the peace she was grateful, yet she felt a sadness around her. Something which was not finished and which would not go away, a state of waiting. She half-expected to hear Joan's rasping breath on the stairs. It was as if Joan and Addie had stepped right back, yet they were still there. As if the silence was alive and needing something more. Something from her.

Shelley looked at herself in the pine mirror in her room. Grey-green eyes, small face and little pointy chin, nose too straight for her own liking with a little cleft between the nostrils, all this hiding behind hair. She polished her gold and black boots carefully. She wouldn't spoil their precious leather in the snow tonight, because they would be inside the clubhouse. She sat by the fire a while to dry her hair, and then went to get dressed.

'Come on, Medusa features,' shouted Adam.

'Medusa nothing! Her hair looks wonderful, Adam,' said her mother. 'People pay hundreds of pounds to have hair that looks like that, they have it coloured and permed and crimped and hot-oiled and God knows what. Her hair is the colour of rich sherry, it's like leaves. Er – you don't think that skirt is too short, love? I thought very short skirts were out?'

Good try, Mother.

Ponderous Dave turned to smile. He refused to be drawn by the skirt. After all, it was little wider then a belt. He wouldn't criticise and he wouldn't warn or be shocked like any self-respecting father-figure.

'Your top is a bit fuzzy, Shelley,' he said unexpectedly. Shelley's top was a silk wool mix, in black. Dave fished in his shirt pocket, which sat to the left of his Dennis the Menace fan club badge and Rolls Royce tie, and handed Shelley something plastic. *Fluff recoverer and shoe horn* it said in flowing green script. *A free gift from Hospitality Hotels.* It worked.

'Don't bend over and show yer bum, Shell, you might get a nasty surprise,' cried Adam. He danced before her, bear-like in his outsize shirt of thick hyacinth-blue cotton, over baggy charcoal trousers. The cuffs reached his finger tips. The colours suited him, she thought reluctantly. He's got that eye for colour that Dad has. Adam grinned, whizzed his eyebrows up and down, hissed, 'But seriously, Matthew'll go mad for you, oh Gorgon without boobies, oh bumpless one.'

'I'm not meeting Matthew,' she said smugly and pushed him out of the way to take her black wool coat and pick her way out across the snow towards Dave's Volvo.

'Right on time, here comes Shuffler,' hissed Adam as they waited for Dave to unlock the car. 'I wonder if he's going to the dance in his dressing-gown?'

It was the old man, slopping down the street. He stopped to look at them, soft-mouthed.

'Good evening, Granddad!' called Adam.

'Don't be cheeky, Adam!' hissed his mother, but the old man raised an arm and his toothless mouth curved into a smile before he set his head forward again and shuffled on.

'His name is Walter Ferane,' said Shelley. 'He's a grave-digger.'

The clubhouse sat by the water's edge, brightly-lit, like a cruise ship against the dark. For Shelley it sparkled with new possibilities and promises of change. Yellow lights danced in the black water as it lapped at the pebbles.

Dave paid for the tickets, peered at them. 'This gives you a binge at the buffet and one drink each,' he said. 'And then after that we have to pay. I'm driving, Clare, so you have my drink and I'll make up for it on the Bulgarian red after we get home. Come on folks. Let's party.'

Across the reception area Shelley saw Matthew with his family. He must have washed his hair and it was wilder than ever, like thousands of dark corkscrews. His mother's hair was neatly set and that must be his father, scrupulously spruce in a grey suit, the trousers a little too short, and hair combed carefully over his weather-beaten scalp. Billy looked well-scrubbed. He and Adam disappeared towards the food.

Matthew sauntered up with that irritating grin. 'Hi, Shelley. Can I get you a drink?' he asked.

'No, Dave's getting me one,' she said. She didn't want to have him cosseting her all evening. The yachtsman might be here.

'Well. Maybe we can dance in a while, though I have to say the band is truly Radio Two.'

He couldn't take a hint, could he? You'd really have to freeze this one right out. She shook her head as if she was denying something to a child. 'I don't feel like dancing, thank you,' she said, and turned away.

Dave brought her orange juice, and she edged her way along

the buffet table, picking at salads and a bread roll. Across the table Adam was scoffing slabs of pizza that he'd swirled with mayonnaise, and talking loudly to Billy at the same time. 'Wow!' he cried, leaping towards the desserts. 'Trifle, and cheesecake, *and* Death by Chocolate!'

If only, thought Shelley, if only. She tiptoed upstairs. The room was wide, with picture windows along two sides, stretching from floor to high ceiling. You could see the boats moored nearby, then beyond that a vast black hole of water.

Matthew was right about the band, she saw. They looked utterly respectable and jolly, no dark and unpredictable depths there. They did have a bass guitarist, but he was Dave's age, with hair thin on the top and lank at the back. They were playing *Love is All Around* in a jaunty fashion. The vocalist had a DJ. Shelley reckoned they would be playing the *Birdy Song* and *Puppet on a String* before they got to *Auld Lang Syne*, but then they decided to play a Pulp song. It was a real mistake.

Most people were still downstairs eating and drinking, as it was early. Shelley glanced covertly at the faces in the dim spaces around the dance floor, but could not see the man from the standing stones. She turned and walked slowly downstairs again.

Mum and Dave were sitting at a table now, close together. Shelley hesitated. She didn't want to join them, but what else could she do?

'You haven't wasted any time, Mum,' she said, looking at the empty glasses on the table.

'I've only had a couple of doubles,' cried her mother. The 's' on the end of doubles sounded more like 'sh' to Shelley. Her mother looked so happy. 'And come to think of it,' she said, turning her glass upside down, 'I'm ready for another one.' Dave rolled his eyes, but took the glass cheerfully. 'Shelley?' he asked, but she shook her head. She didn't want alcohol tonight. She didn't need anything.

'Enjoying yourself, love?'

Shelley shrugged. There was a pause. Then she said, 'We don't have many photos of New Year and Christmas when Dad was with us, do we?'

Her mother sat up stiffly, bracing herself.

'I mean, in my album. I've plenty of you and me and Adam, but Dad's never there.'

'Leave it, Shelley,' said her mother quietly, but Shelley could not. It was as if she had a needle but was addicted to the piercing, to the giving of the injection, rather than whatever drug was in it.

'There are pictures of my birthday parties. I'm six in one, 'cos it says so on the cake, and maybe seven or eight in the next one. You're in one, and the Unspeakable is showing off in another. There's no Dad in the picture.'

In the dimness of the room her mother's eyes grew huge and glistening. She turned them to search desperately for Dave, but he was queueing at the bar.

'Why have we no photos of me and my father together?' persisted Shelley. 'There should be, on my birthday, not just me and Adam, and me and you.'

Her mother put her hand over her eyes.

'Come on, couldn't you be bothered to take any for me?' cried Shelley. 'Why aren't there any photos of me and Dad?'

Her mother gave a sort of shudder. 'Because he isn't yours,' she muttered.

A moment passed. Shelley felt as if the room had flown away from her, and she was sitting in some dark, high place. She saw below her the people, all the mouths moving, making words but no noise, a crowd of chatterers, heads thrown back in silent laughter.

'Declan isn't your father,' said her mother again.

'What? Not mine? But . . . is he Adam's father?'

'Yes.'

'If . . . if Declan isn't mine, then who is?' Shelley whispered.

Her mother took her hand away from her forehead. Her face twitched as if she was in pain.

'I don't know.'

Twelve

Shelley stood up, turned and dream-walked across the room. She saw that Matthew walked a little ahead of her, with a girl she didn't recognise. They turned and climbed the stairs. To dance, she supposed. Shelley wanted to call out to him, but she could not, and he wouldn't want to hear her. No, she would go beyond the wall of glass, rimmed with the reflections of the lights, out to the night.

She stopped by the cloakroom. The attendant stared at her.

'It's that one,' Shelley said, pointing to her coat. She turned and walked towards the doors.

'Hello,' said a voice. 'Don't I know you?'

She looked up at him, from eyes that felt as if they hurt. She had seen him before. He had pale hair, angel's hair, eyes blue as the sea in Greece. It was the yachtsman, but he was different tonight.

'You're not going out there are you?' he said. She saw that his face was pink, and his sea eyes were smeared with blood, and somehow swollen.

'I'll come with you,' he said. 'I'll come for a walk with you,' and he put his face down to hers so that she could smell that smell; drink, drink on an unfamiliar skin, and see between his wet lips a glimpse of his tongue.

'No,' she cried and wrenched her arm away. 'No!'

Shelley struggled with the glass doors. She didn't know where she was going, only that it was away, and she must hurry for he was following. She let the heavy doors swing back, perhaps it would knock him away. She glanced over her shoulder, not yet, he's not there yet, but she must run. The cold hit her face hard.

Shelley hurried along the water's edge, taking herself away from the hurt. She was humiliated, like a young child dismissed by the adults. Turned out of their world, turned away by their actions and decisions. Turned out by her mother and Declan, and Dave, and Matthew, and now this foul lie of a man with his angel hair. Hot tears welled and spilled down her face. It was even worse than before. She was a fatherless child.

Mum must be wrong. She was like Declan, she was artistic, she loved books and poetry as he did, he *must* be her father... but if he wasn't, who was? And who was she? Shelley on her own.

It always came to the same point. Being alone. Life never got any further on. Now she did not even have a father. Not even a father who had left her. Her father did not even know she existed.

She turned towards the waiting water. It sat, motionless, black as pitch. She wanted to wade out into it and just disappear, for everything to stop, but she knew she couldn't stand the cold.

'I'll head up to the mine again,' she told herself. 'That's the plan. I know that's where I'm supposed to go. That's where Addie hid.'

Her hand in its coat pocket felt that little shape again, the piece of mineral. The Blue John. Perhaps the Blue John was bad luck, some terrible talisman of misfortune. She would put it back in the mine where she had found it.

'It's not mine,' she cried. 'Nothing is.'

She could stay up there, no one would find her, she wouldn't have to face things. It could all just end in a great cold blankness. The lights from the buildings did not reach this far. If it wasn't for the luminosity of the snow she would not have seen which was land and which was water. They flowed into each other, she could hear them flowing.

The hills were ghostly with snow. That hill on the left, that was the right one, she was sure. The village lay on the other side. She glanced back up at the sky. There was a moon tonight, only it was masked by cloud, like the blood spread across his gibbous eye.

She was beginning to find the darkness oppressive, and there were those cries again. It wouldn't be birds, not at night. No, the cries must be from the clubhouse, the people there enjoying themselves, belonging in their families and their groups. Or owls, perhaps, little owls whistling to mark their territory, crying as they flew to their boundaries, as they sensed their homes.

Shelley suddenly thought of her boots, of what a terrible water mark there would be on the leather. These were expensive fashion boots, not the sort to hike over snowy hills in Derbyshire. Too bad. Who cared what she looked like?

She wasn't walking on snow now. The snow must be melting, and she was walking on roughness. A cinder path. It was now too dark to see where land ended and water began. If only the moon would come out! She was walking on liquid mud, she was still low down, and she wanted to get high up by the mine and the Mohican coxcomb of trees. She felt thin, like a needle. She was a needle to give pain, and the needle of a compass, drawn to the hill. The mine drew her to it, pulled her towards its mouth. She shut her eyes and ploughed forward. And then she was under!

She gasped, mouth filled, nose smothered, she gulped and floundered. All black. Her feet touched something soft, then away again, she hit and pushed at the water to leave her alone. It was so cold! Bone-cold, it made her gasp, she mustn't, she'd swallow the water, up to the top, there was a moon, a light, then down again, but it wasn't all dark now, there were shapes that ebbed and swelled with the water.

Shelley watched herself drowning. She saw her heavy coat pull her down, saw herself struggle with the weight of icy water, heard it bubble far away, but in her ears, like the filter in Adam's aquarium. She saw Adam, the little boy, Adam called to her, 'Shell!' She knew it was that, although she didn't hear the word.

And then she heard them. All around her, flowing and skimming around her head, the sea creatures from millions of years ago, the fossils in the limestone, the wash and ebb and pull of the warm oceans, pulling at her now. A vast creature turning like an earthquake in the hill, roaring. The deafening cracking of ice. The terrible violence to the earth, the smashing and breaking and gouging out of it by men, as if they dragged out huge teeth of rock from tender gums that filled at once with blood. The bellow of a bull and the bleat of a bloated sheep in the water. Shouts and steeple bells from the drowned valley. She heard the rattling bones from a burial chamber at Slipperlow, heard the call of a crouching child buried in rock and the singing of a family in a cave. The tramp of the Romans marching up the street north of the village. A pick hammering at lead. Gunpowder. Tapping in the rock. Knocking underground. She heard the cries of men covered by rushing earth, and the weeping of their wives, the wail of a baby and the keening of all the mothers who have lost their children. She heard the moans of a girl, a girl she knew, dying behind the stairs, and the frightened breathing of another girl dragged from the mine shaft.

Around her swarmed voices and stories, snippets, episodes like wraiths whirling around her head, louder and louder, painfully loud, all calling, 'Listen! Hear me!' And then a little stone man whirled past, hand over his heart, and she saw that he was smiling at her. 'Shelley!' she heard. 'Shelley, it's all right. We've got you!'

The boom of water. Then silence. Deafening silence.

Thirteen

Cold, the room was so cold, after its empty evening. Dave knelt in front of the fire, easing the logs apart with the poker, so that the flames billowed between them.

Shelley stared at Adam. He was so strange. She looked down and saw that she was wrapped in a blanket, her hair wound in a towel.

'Where's Mum?' she asked. 'Where's Mum?'

Dave sat back on his heels. He wiped his forehead, then turned to her a face ploughed up in worry. 'I don't know,' he said. 'I don't know, Shelley. I spent a while getting drinks. By the time I got back she had gone, with my keys off the table.'

'Oh.' Her teeth were chattering.

'Trouble is,' said Dave, 'she's legless. She's no good at driving in the snow anyway. And she's had way over the limit.'

The Volvo would be overturned at the bottom of the steep hill out of the village. That was it. Mum would be trapped in there. Unconscious. Bleeding. Freezing. Dead.

'Get dressed, Adam,' said Dave.

Shelley looked at Adam again and finally realised now what was odd about him. He stood in front of the fire in only his red underpants. His shivering legs looked white and thin, and fine dark hairs Shelley hadn't noticed before sprouted around his knees and shins, as if they were trying to keep him warm above the goose pimples.

'What are you doing, Adam?' she asked.

'Warming my bum, of course. I always strip off for fun about this time of year.' He tried to grin at her through his shivering, yet she saw that his face was drained white from fear. 'I saw you sweeping out, Shelley,' he said. 'I was just moving in on some profiteroles. I could tell you were upset. Didn't you hear me call you?'

'No.'

'On purpose, I thought. Flouncer. So I went to find Matthew. He said you'd be doing a snooty Greta Garbo turn. Then we see you heading for some drunk berk in a posey white suit. We didn't like that, so we followed, but you'd stormed out. Followed, not too close. Didn't want my head bitten off. Then all of a sudden you were in there, Shelley. God, I was terrified. Matthew said the kiss of life was fun, anyway.'

'He didn't!' she cried.

'That's right, he didn't. You were spewing up the second we dragged you out. Like those cartoon characters when they throw up tadpoles and frogs. You were like a sea monster, Nessie in high heels. Give my sister the kiss of life? The very idea, ugh!'

Of course, he doesn't know, does he, thought Shelley. I am his half-sister. Half-sister. Nothing more.

'I think Matthew was quite disappointed you didn't need the kiss,' he said. 'Where did you think you were off to, Shelley?'

'The mine at the top of the hill,' she said.

'No, not at night, love, not up there,' said Dave. 'It can be dangerous, especially in this weather. You'd slip. Or get drowned when the snow melted.' There was a pause. 'Dangerous. As you discovered,' he said.

'Anyway, I'm off to find more clothes,' muttered Adam and wandered off.

'Where's Mum?' she said again.

'You must have had a row,' said Dave, coming over to her.

'No. She told me,' whispered Shelley. 'About my father. Or lack of father.'

'She hasn't known how to tell you, love,' said Dave. 'She should have told you years ago, but she couldn't and I can see why, and I know how she's suffered.'

The door burst open and in fell Shelley's mum, with Matthew close behind. She saw Shelley and lurched across the room to her, wrapping her in cold arms. 'I thought I'd lost you,' she whimpered. 'I thought you'd gone.'

Shelley clung to her mother, wanting to push her hard away, but she clung to her like a raft, feeling the tears streaming and coursing down her cheeks. She heard an echo in her head of Addie's sad voice, 'she does not beg me back to her hearthside ...'

Well this mother does, thought Shelley. She whispered, 'Are *you* mine?'

Her mother drew back and stared at her. 'Yes I am,' she said. 'One hundred per cent. I always will be. I'm sorry that's all I can ever say to you, Shelley. I should have told you years ago, but every time I tried, I just couldn't. I've been so worried! You're going away soon, and I hadn't told you. I'm going to miss you so much anyway.'

'Oh,' murmured Shelley. That's what she'd overheard that morning when she came back from setting her skylark, her mother worrying that she'd leave home before she knew.

Her mother wiped her eyes with the back of her hand. 'Sometimes you seem to – to feel so badly towards me. I just couldn't take your rejection.'

And I could never take yours, said Shelley. But not aloud. She asked fearfully, 'Who was he?'

'Oh . . . Shelley . . . he was someone I met at a party when I was a student. When I was a little drunk. When I didn't believe such things could happen. He had beautiful curly hair. Like yours, of course. That's all I remember. I'm so sorry. It was too easy and silly, and of course nowadays you lot are all so clever, and you would never have unprotected sex, and it would never happen. But I am not ashamed or sorry, because something marvellous came from those few unconscious seconds, Shelley. You.'

It's just so weird, Mum, I feel as if it's a story about a friend, not my own mother. You've always seemed so . . . . so . . . '

'Sensible? In charge? Old? I'm sorry. But from the very second

I sensed I was pregnant, I also knew I could never lose you. All that woman's right to choose abortion bit, I've always supported it, but it's for other women, not me.'

'So what about – Declan?'

'I met Declan almost immediately, before I even realised I was having you.'

'And did Declan know he wasn't my father?'

'Yes. But it wouldn't have made any difference if he had been your natural father. He couldn't show you love, somehow. He always said that you were too imaginative, too clever for happiness. Especially for a girl. Yes, he said that. He thought you'd be unstable. And he wasn't very loving to Adam, you know.'

'Why not?'

'He's just not that sort of man. Some people aren't. But he didn't want anyone else to know you weren't his daughter. Pride, in some weird way. In case people thought I had made a cuckold out of him, I suppose.' Her mother sighed, painfully. 'And Adam thought it was all my fault his father had gone, and some of it was of course. It's understandable,' she said and sighed. 'Anything is understandable, Shelley.'

'No, not anything, Mum. Does Adam know?'

'No. Shall I tell him now?'

'No,' said Shelley thoughtfully. 'I'll tell him sometime.'

'You know, Shelley, it was you who comforted Adam after Declan ran out on us,' said her mother. 'It was you Adam needed. You never realised that, did you?'

110

Dave came back with a pot of tea and mugs on a tray. Matthew followed behind with packets of biscuits.

He was saying, 'Don't worry, I'll get the Land-Rover to it in the morning. Poor old Volvo, stuck in a drift.' He looked long at Shelley, then he said, 'You *are* a daft little cow. No good in cable cars, and then you go looking for a mine to fall down, and almost drown instead. Are you putting yourself through some sort of elemental testing?' He grinned. 'Have a biscuit and come back to us,' he said.

Dave suddenly threw himself down in a chair, took off his glasses and wiped his eyes with his Rolls Royce tie. Shelley stared. He was red-faced, worried sick. This wasn't the usual calm koala. He looked at Shelley and said, 'Don't do that again. You're the nearest thing to a daughter I've got. I love you. And I love your mum, and I don't want her hurt.'

Adam bounced back into the room, in a jumper and cords. Now Shelley noticed that the whiteness of his face was blotched. He had been crying. He looked like a little boy.

'I'd have come for a walk with you if you'd wanted, Shell,' he said. 'I could have life-saved you. Why did you go?'

'She felt bad, didn't you, Shelley?' said Dave gently. 'Lonely, I guess. But, Shelley, there are no such things as groups. They're not true. Always remember that. There's just people on their own, pretending. We try to be together, it makes us feel strong. Sometimes we manage it and sometimes we don't.'

'Shelley,' said her mother. 'Shelley, you didn't – you – you didn't mean to – ' she began.

'No, of course I didn't mean to,' said Shelley. 'It was daft, I know, I was just a bit beyond it, and it was so dark, and I somehow fell in.' She sat up. 'Mum, it was quite extraordinary,' she said. 'You can't imagine what I heard. I heard them all, all the voices round the rocks.'

'There, there,' her mother smiled and stroked the back of Shelley's hand with soft fingers. 'How are you feeling, love?'

'Bewildered,' said Shelley. 'And sort of new.'

Fourteen

Adam sprinkled sugar methodically over his Weetabix, then laid the spoon beside his bowl. He looked at Shelley with admiration.

'So you're my half-sister?' he said. 'I can't believe it of Mum. Imagining any of them having sex is bad enough, but irresponsible sex out of fun . . . it's unthinkable. And . . . we really don't know who your father is?'

'No. I could choose any father in the world,' Shelley said, wryly.

'Just think, Shell, you could be little Miss Schwarzenegger, or Salmanette Rushdie, or – or – a John Majorette! Aaagh!'

'Thank you very much, Adam.'

He frowned. He said, 'Does it make you feel strange, Shelley?'

'Yes. Very strange. I feel as if I'm splitting right out of an old shell. In a way it's given me a kind of freedom. I can be who I like. I don't have to think I'm trapped by what my parents are. I mean, I'm bound to have some of Mum in me, but I feel as if I have at least fifty per cent sheer licence.'

They giggled.

She said, 'But it also makes me frightened. Not knowing what you have in you is a bit frightening. Fun frightening, though. I'm like a kite that's had its string cut.'

'And just think, you can't hate your little brother in quite the same way, because I'm not!'

Shelley smiled at him, reached for the marmalade. He was right. Already he looked different to her. He wasn't such a millstone. He looked quite attractive. 'You look much more human now you're not my full brother,' she said, truthfully.

'You're too kind, Shelley. Well. I'm cold. I'm taking me Weeties back to bed,' he said, and went upstairs.

I'll have to get to know him all over again, thought Shelley.

There was a knock at the front door. Before Shelley could drag herself up out of the chair to answer it, her mother appeared and opened the door. It was Mrs Harvey.

'Matthew's just dropped me off,' she said. 'He's on his way down in the Land-Rover to pull your man's car out.' The two women sniggered. 'It would be you who got stuck,' said Mrs Harvey. 'It's never them, is it? It's like it's always me who leaves the gate open so the cows get out. Anyway, it'll be easy now. It's thawing.'

Shelley could hear the streams of snow water coursing down the cobbles to the bottom of the hill and, shielding her eyes against the sunlight that streamed in through the doorway, she saw big refracted drops gather and fall from the roof-edge opposite, and then a great rush of snow slipping down the cat-slide roof on to the road.

114

She felt her spirits lift and lighten this morning.

Her mum brought Mrs Harvey in and offered her coffee.

'That'd be lovely. And how are you today, Shelley? Matt has been worried sick about you, he really has. I know when he goes quiet it's something serious.'

'Can't imagine Matthew being quiet,' said Shelley.

'Oh, it doesn't happen often,' said Mrs Harvey, smiling indulgently as she thought of her son. 'I must say, you look well, duck. A bit tired, but you look better than you did the last time I saw you. You were a touch preoccupied, I think.'

'Maybe,' said Shelley.

'Matthew was asking me about, er, what's happened in the cottage and that. He said you had an awareness.'

'You could call it that,' said Shelley. 'I've been worried, though. I feel as if I've been left up in the air.'

'How do you mean?'

'Well, I've had to listen to the stories of two girls. Reluctantly at first, but now their voices have withdrawn I feel sad, as if I miss them. And the stories just stop. I don't really know the end. I think one of them died, after she'd borne a dead baby.'

'Is it the one here? The one under the stairs?' asked Mrs Harvey.

'Yes! Did you listen to her?'

'I didn't have much option when I was living here, the way she ranted on. She made me feel bad. Frank's old granny told me once there was a girl who just disappeared when she was only thirteen. A girl who was a bit simple . . . this girl's own mother died giving birth to her. No records. Makes you wonder if she ever did exist. Sad, isn't it? Mind you, life was cheap then. They died as babies, they died in childbirth too. And Frank's granny said that the Harveys haven't been too good with their girls in the past. This one really ranted. But I could never understand what she was saying. You must be a better listener than me, Shelley. Tell you what, you're nearer her age. She would have been better talking to you.'

'Poor Joan,' said Shelley. 'Poor unhappy Joan.'

'So, Joan's the smelly one under the stairs, is she?' said Shelley's mum, setting down a cafetiere of coffee on the table.

'Well, yes, Joan is somewhere round there,' she said. 'How did you know, Mum? You can't hear her can you?'

'No, love. It wasn't me who supplied you with that talent. Not my genes, dear. I just knew you'd got a voice there, that's all. I know when you're not with us, I always have. I'm maybe a little bit jealous. You never took notice of me like that.'

'I never told you about hearing these things, Mum. I told Declan and he said it was a bad idea, that people would think I was ill, schizophrenic, if I let on that I heard stuff from the spirit world. Or whatever you want to call it. But you weren't supposed to know about the voices, Mum.'

'I realise that,' said her mother, pulling a mock hurt face. 'But it's fairly obvious to me when you've clocked off from here and now and are plugged in to a voice with no body.'

Mrs Harvey said, 'You've got a daughter with a gift, Mrs – er – '

'Clare. Yes, I know. I have wondered about renting her out, or putting her on TV. But she's a bit stroppy. You may have noticed.'

'Matthew said you were drawn to the mine, Shelley,' said Mrs Harvey. 'There was a girl lost up there. They hunted her down for sheep-stealing in the eighteenth century. It's all covered up in the mists of time. Anyway, I never listened to that one, I've always kept well away from the mine. It gives me the creeps! And it's a good job another girl wasn't lost down the mine last night.'

Shelley smiled, reached for her mum's hand, gave it a gentle squeeze.

Adam burst out of the stairwell. 'Look at you lot, hunched over that cafetiere,' he said. 'When shall we three meet again?'

The window to the street darkened as the Land-Rover chugged to park, and they heard the engine of the Volvo just behind.

'Put the kettle on for Matt and Dave, love,' said Mum to Adam. 'So, Shelley. Was your mine girl a sheep-stealer?'

'No,' she said. She thought, I fear she was hanged, and for a crime she did not commit. I miss the voices. They have made me part of something much greater, not just my own mind. I have shared their sadness and acknowledged it. And after all, I didn't get raped or hanged. I've got off lightly. I need to tell my story now. Don't know if anyone will listen or not.

Shelley did go back to the mine again. She knew she should, not with Matthew, although he wanted to come with her, but alone.

So Shelley sat and told her story, in her head, the story of her growing up, hoping that there was an awareness of it back across the years, to Addie Johnson and to Joan. She told them of her mother and brother, and Declan and Dave, and of coming here to Matthew and the cottage and the mine, and of almost drowning. She told this story with its bizarre but not unhappy ending into the wound in the hillside.

She held the Blue John butterfly wing in her hand. At one time, the night of her near drowning, she had thought to put this back, but now she knew that she must keep it. A gift from a loving father to his dear daughter. She would keep it safe on Addie's behalf. Something of that real love would be salvaged. Shelley did not know her real father, and would not try to find him. All that was past. But dear Dave would do as a stand-in.

Now Shelley looked forward to moving to the new house. She knew that voices waited for her there, but these would be from the future, perhaps even the voice of her own daughter.

She stood up, brushed the snow off her coat, ready.

And I, Addie Johnson, left my childhood in the mine.

I was taken on a cart to the town of Derby, and confined in Derby gaol awaiting my trial and my condemnation, there being no House of Correction.

Now the year was 1770 and sheep-stealing was a capital offence. I welcomed the dream of death although I feared that moment of the cap over my face and the rope tight about my neck.

I saw no one but my fellow prisoners, crammed

together as we were. There was a baker who wore his own slank hair, and had sold underweight bread, two miners who had stolen the smallest quantity of lead ore and a thick-talking woman who was a thief, I am sure of it, though she denied this all day and all night. I learned much of their lives from them, their lives of want. I told them nothing in return. Who would listen?

Then came the Quarter Sessions. They would not hang me. The Justice said that I was young, must think on my crime. I was to be transported as soon as might be convenient to His Majesty's colonies in America for seven years. A few years more, and I would have been shut up in a hulk on the river Thames, for in 1775, England and America were at war.

First to Liverpool. We were delivered there after some days in a merchant's wagon. The booming cathedral bells and swarming of folk in the streets was a terror to me, used as I was only to the uplands, but there was worse to come. My greatest punishment was the sea. I had never seen or even dreamed of such a thing! It was a restless, greedy beast, that smelled so strong and was so fierce and without end or mercy, and all my chained companions screamed and begged forgiveness for their crimes.

At last, the land came to us. A foreign land. America. I worked my sentence as a servant girl. I never could, nor indeed wished, to return to England, I had left the child in me behind there, I would not think of it, or them.

After some years I felt my skin much healed! It was grown soft as moss, healed from its pitted roughness. My beloved father had always promised me that it would heal itself one day, and now it did.

I had washed my skin in May dew from the hawthorn every spring, and in holy wells, but all to no avail. I had put my trust in candles and ash trees. No more. I put no faith in superstition now. And indeed, I wondered at God's fairness. He was a bewilderment to me. As you may see, I was much changed.

Later I was married with Thomas Campbell, a good man, a farmer. I learned again to love, and in time I had two children. First a boy. We named him Thomas. Three years later I had another child. This time my baby was a girl. I loved her none the less because of it.

A Selected List of Fiction from Mammoth

While every effort is made to keep prices low, it is sometimes necessary to increase prices at short notice. Mandarin Paperbacks reserves the right to show new retail prices on covers which may differ from those previously advertised in the text or elsewhere.

The prices shown below were correct at the time of going to press.

All these books are available at your bookshop or newsagent, or can be ordered direct from the address below. Just tick the titles you want and fill in the form below.

Cash Sales Department, PO Box 5, Rushden, Northants NN10 6YX.
Fax: 01933 414047 : Phone: 01933 414000.

Please send cheque, payable to 'Reed Book Services Ltd.', or postal order for purchase price quoted and allow the following for postage and packing:

£1.00 for the first book, 50p for the second; **FREE POSTAGE AND PACKING FOR THREE BOOKS OR MORE PER ORDER.**

NAME (Block letters)..

ADDRESS ....

....

☐ I enclose my remittance for...........................

☐ I wish to pay by Access/Visa Card Number

Expiry Date

Signature...

Please quote our reference: MAND